The Papers of Matthew Locke

John Wheatley

The Papers of Matthew Locke

All rights reserved. No part of this production may be reproduced, stored in a retrieval system, or transmitted in any form or by any means, electronic, mechanical, photocopy, recording or otherwise, without permission of the copyright owner. Nor can it be circulated in any form of binding or cover other than that in which is published and without similar condition including this condition being imposed on a subsequent purchaser. `The Papers of Matthew Locke` is a work of historical fiction. The characters bear no relation to any persons, living or dead.

Copyright © 2012 John Wheatley

ISBN: 1475059493
ISBN-13:9781475059496

Cover photograph `The Beach at Lleiniog, Anglesey`
by Lesley Bowers

For my son, Daniel

1982 - 2011

PREFACE

Whether my great-grandfather, Matthew Locke, whose papers are here presented, ever read *The Mabinogion*, or knew of its existence, I have no way of knowing. I am told by my wife, who is a teacher of Literature at Trinity College, that the collection of tales which go by that name, deriving from Welsh manuscripts of the eleventh century, or thereabouts, first appeared in English translation in a publication commissioned by Lady Charlotte Guest in the mid-nineteenth century, so it was certainly extant during his lifetime, but beyond that it is difficult to say. It was my wife who pointed out that certain references in my great grandfather's text – things which to me had seemed merely obscure and bizarre – mirrored events in one of the so-called *branches* of *the Mabinogion*, or, as she put it, contained narrative elements that can be traced in *the Mabinogi,* though, not necessarily deriving directly from it. When I asked her to clarify this distinction, she explained that the tales recorded in medieval Welsh, though no doubt containing some contemporary literary invention, are, in some cases at least, only versions of tales that go back, in oral tradition, possibly as far back as the bronze age [when, she pointed out, for my edification, the stories recorded in the Iliad and the Odyssey have their origins] and that, like those famous tales, they may well have derived from events which actually took place in the dim and distant past.

My great-grandfather retired to a small cottage in Anglesey in 1923, leaving the large family house in Dublin for the use of his son, my grandfather, and his young family. My father took over the house in 1948, ten years before I was born, and I inherited it, in turn, when my father died in 2003. Like many large houses which have been in the same family for many generations, it was full of accumulated lumber, and it was when my wife and I decided finally to sell the house five years later, that my great-grandfather's manuscript was discovered.

It is handwritten, on sheets of plain paper, in an even though slightly sloping writing, and a colleague of my wife, in the department of Linguistics and Palaeography, has suggested that it was probably written within a fairly short space of time, though there is some evidence, apparently, even from a casual inspection of the ink and handwriting, that the first chapter, and the quotation from *The Tempest* which precedes it, together with the subheading of Part 2 - *The White Raven* - were added later. At the beginning of the manuscript, there is a sheet whose contents are repeated later. Whether or not this was intentional, or simply a corrected sheet which was not discarded, we do not know; but in the interest of presenting the manuscript and its order as it was originally found, this sheet has been included as a *prelude*.

The *Chapter* and *Part* numbers have been added, for the reader's convenience, by my wife, who prepared the text for publication, though in so doing she was guided by my great-grandfather's fairly consistent habits in terms of turning over a sheet, or starting a new sheet altogether. There is no date on the manuscript, though several sheets on similar paper and with similar writing, found in the same chest, relate to family business interests in Java, and it is known that my great-grandfather spent some periods of time there in the 1880s.

A little research on the internet confirmed two shipwrecks which my great-grandfather mentions [it had long been a story in the family, fanciful I always thought, that he had been marooned on the Welsh coast as a young man] those of the *Norman Court* and the *Charming Jenny*.

It was also possible to ascertain, that two Roman legions under Suetonius Paulinus crossed to *Insula Mona* [Anglesey] from the mainland in AD 60 with the express intention of destroying the Druidic culture and the political menace it represented in the eyes of the administrators and generals of the *Pax Romana*.

Interestingly, there are also several easily accessed website references to *Bedd Branwen*, an ancient burial chamber whose remnants can still be found in a farmer's field near Llandeusant in Anglesey.

Prelude

The girl knew he was following her, but he did not know whether or not she was afraid. As they entered the village, she quickened her pace, and it was difficult to keep track of her as she made her way through the clusters of dwellings. Only once she looked back, and their eyes met in recognition. Then she hurried on again, and when he came to the corner where she had turned just a moment before, she was entering the gate of a palisade surrounding more substantial buildings. He hurried across the cleared space in front of the palisade, but as he reached the gateway, the heavy oak doors, embossed with metal studs, were already closing, and a moment later, he heard the sound of the solid wooden bolts sliding into place.

Part One

The Loss of the Norman Court

Now would I give a thousand furlongs of sea for an acre of barren ground, long heath, brown furze, any thing. The wills above be done! but I would fain die a dry death.

The Tempest

Chapter 1

The *Norman Court*, bound for Greenock on the Firth of Clyde, and laden with a thousand tons of sugar from Jacarta, was wrecked off the west coast of Anglesey on the 29th March, 1883. Sister ship to *The Cutty Sark,* and amongst the fastest traders of the day, she had been engaged in the China Trade, recording a best passage of 94 days from Macao to the Lizard in 1872, before new owners, Baine and Johnson, set her to the Java sugar trade in 1881.

On the final stages of her homeward journey, through St George's Channel, she was running with a strong south westerly which by mid-afternoon had blown into a full gale. She passed Bardsey Island, and on the approach to Holyhead, in worsening visibility, was driven off course, and despite the captain's best efforts to turn her about, she was blown broadside on, and ran aground on the submerged rocks of Cymyran Bay, between Ynys Feurig, known as Starvation Island, and Rhoscolyn, and as night approached, battered by a raging sea, she began to break up.

The first light revealed, to folk gathering on the shore at the news of a wreck, a desperate scene. The ship was listing towards the shore at a crazy angle, her main mast broken, with twenty foot waves surging around her. Men clung to the rigging, some waving and shouting, others hanging, seemingly lifeless, like flies caught in a spider's web.

No strangers to the savagery of their own coastal waters, the people of Anglesey had spent half a century building systems of rescue and prevention: the lighthouses at South Stack, Lynas Point, Penmon, the Skerries; the lifeboat houses at Moelfre, Holyhead, Rhoscolyn, Beaumaris. On this occasion, however, the nearest lifeboat, at Rhoscolyn, was in Treaddur undergoing repairs, and out of service. On the shore, the villagers attempted to fire rescue lines, but the rockets were feeble in the high blustery wind, and they were blown aside or fell miserably short. Standing to their waists in the freezing surf, men and women tried to steady a local boat as it attempted to brave the surf and reach the beleaguered ship, but drawing close, a terrific wave tossed the boat high and then filled it with water. One man, thrown overboard, only survived by catching a line and hanging on until his fellows pulled him back aboard. The boat was driven back onto the shore, its crew exhausted.

Meantime, Colonel Marshall of the Rhoscolyn lifeboatmen had sent word to Holyhead, and a train was chartered to bring a boat and crew in a last ditch attempt to save the men of the *Norman Court*. Disembarking from the train, the Holyhead men carried their boat a mile across open ground, and managed to launch at Rhosneigr and board the broken ship. Twenty men were rescued. Two had died from exposure. It was said that the men they rescued were so numb that they had to prized from the rigging like frozen washing.

Chapter 2

It was some time, not just hours, but days and weeks before I fully understood what had happened to me. To begin with, my waking consciousness, if such it might be called, was as troubled and dislocated as the fractured dreams whose images shifted and tumbled headlong as in a kaleidoscope.

They say that sometimes, for hours on end, I chattered like a jackdaw, making no sense at all, and oblivious as to whether or not I had a listener; at other times I maintained a total silence, staring unblinkingly into the distance as if I saw some terror there that held me in a trance.

The first clear memory that came back to me was that of being aware, as my rescuers unfastened me, that my wrist had been tied to the rigging by a red bandanna, and I am certain now that had it not been for that act of care, I would have plunged to my death in the thrashing sea long before rescue came.

I learned later that in the first confusion, after we had hit the reef, I was struck across the shoulder and the back of the head by a falling spar from the mainmast, though to this day my memory of that incident has remained a blank page, only the bruising, changing from ink black to lurid purple and yellow, remaining, for many weeks, as evidence of its having happened. It was, from what I can piece together, by all accounts, a near escape from death.

I joined the *Norman Court,* at my father's instigation, at Jacarta, having spent five months in Indonesia, visiting the sugar plantations, making myself fit, as he saw it, to take my place in the world of commerce in which he, and his own father in turn, had made it their business to excel. My lack of enthusiasm for that sphere of human endeavour made me something of a disappointment to him, I fear, and, following my mother's death – I was twenty at the time - he was glad to be rid of me, hoping, I'm sure, that exposure to the world would knock some sense into me.

There are somewhere in the region of thirty sugar estates on Java, controlled mainly by the Dutch. By its nature, the production of sugar is labour intensive, the crop being too heavy to ship in its raw form. At the time of my visit, mechanisation had made few inroads, and the picking and crushing was still largely carried out by hand. Harsh conditions are imposed on the native labourers, and the migrant workers, largely Chinese, for little reward to improve their own lives beyond bare subsistence. There were times, I admit, when, observing the poor living conditions and diet of the workforce, I was moved to reflect that all their efforts are for the sake of a delicacy - such a fashion in Europe - whose products, cakes, sticky coated pastries and glazed sweets are entirely unknown to their own children. When I expressed my sense of this anomaly in letters to my father, he had little patience with me, needless to say. He made the point very firmly that sentiment has no place in business, and that if the lot of the natives is to be improved, it must be through the prosperity they are enabled to create.

The *Norman Court* was, fully rigged and under sail, a magnificent sight to behold, and to be on board as she sliced through the Indian Ocean was, at first, a thrilling experience. But I am not a natural sailor. On the passage out, despite conditions which were generally considered to be clement, it was several days before I came anywhere near to finding my sea-legs. I had never imagined, except as they are described in poetry, such tempestuous seas as were to beset us, on the homeward journey, as we rounded the Cape and sailed northward, but there were days when, for several hours together, I was so racked with the sea-sickness that I could well have wished myself dead.

I was, of course, roundly mocked by the men of the ship's crew, not maliciously, but enough to deflate the pride of a young man, for all young men like to think themselves the equal of their fellows. There was one member of the crew, a Corsican, Paolo, who at first I feared more than the others, perhaps because I didn't fully understand his dialect, and who I therefore suspected, unreasonably, of making jibes. He it was, however, who became, as the journey progressed, my protector, and I understood - though the seafaring community is generally a cosmopolitan one - that he, too, felt like an outsider. In his faltering English, he explained to me that a man's prowess is not in his comparisons with other men, but in his truthfulness to himself, a truthfulness that will ultimately be tested on its own terms. They were words which, later, I had good reason to remember.

    As my memories began to return, I recalled that we had to climb onto the rigging to escape the waves which were breaking over the deck of the ship, and I remember slipping in and out of consciousness, and experiencing, with the wash of the occasionally mountainous breakers over my head, a calm acceptance that I was going to drown. The cold stings at first, but then you lose sensation, feeling a sense of well-being, perhaps welcoming the certainty of approaching death.

    The red bandanna which saved my life belonged, of course, to Paolo. In his business about the ship, he was never without it, but at some moment, he had chosen to use it as a means of securing me to the rigging when, as he must have been aware, I had no means of protecting myself.

    I also learned that it was he who had left money with the people in Rhosneigr, to look after me, and, later, that he had gone through the shipping line to contact my father in Dublin, and make my situation known to him. I had never seen him without his bandanna, and, funnily enough, could not imagine him without it. Whether or not I will ever see him again in this life, I do not know, for men of the sea are men who disperse to the four corners of the earth; however, one always keeps open the hope that long lost friends will one day cross our paths again so that we can share the recollection of times past, and say our thanks where no thanks could be said at the time. If I say however, that I have already seen him, not in this world but in some other where I have been and which I don't comprehend, that is possibly the true point at which this story begins.

Chapter 3

I was brought, more dead than alive, to the house of Llwys Llywellyn in Rhosneiger, not more than half a mile from the spot where the *Norman Court*, still visible, as it was to be for many years, had foundered.

Llwys himself was an old man, white haired and gracious, though he had somewhat lost the rule of his house to his nephew, Evan, hot tempered and loud mouthed, and with an opinion on everything, including the wisdom of keeping a helpless invalid in the house, a stranger who required almost constant nursing. On this point, however, Llwys was not to be countermanded. From most matters of family business, he withdrew - preferring to busy himself with his books, and with his bees, both occupations in which he took great pleasure - allowing Evan to rule the roost, but when he took a stand on a matter of principle, and he regarded hospitality as a principle of the highest importance, his authority was not to be denied.

Evan was, by trade, a blacksmith, having served his indentures a full seven years from the age of twelve, and he was now twenty three, a little older than myself.

There were two daughters of the house, Bryony, who was the daughter of Llwys's first marriage, and Megan, his daughter to a second wife, now also dead. Evan was his sister's son, and he had always lived under Llwys' roof, his mother having died in childbirth and his father being unknown.

Bryony was known in the village as the quiet daughter of Llwys, sometimes the unhappy one, Llwys' sorrowful daughter; Megan, on the other hand, was vain and pretty, with a liking for trinkets and ribbons, and an equal dislike for chores or any kind of household duty that would get her hands dirty or force her to wear clothes that were for work rather than adornment.

It was Bryony who I came to think of as my nurse. She was a moody girl, preoccupied, uncommunicative, as though some gloomy shadow hung perpetually over her life. But as a nurse she was attentive and careful. In truth, to begin with, I was aware of her only in the few lucid intervals I had, but when I was too weak even to feed myself, she sat by the side of the bed, patiently, with a spoon and a bowl of broth, waiting for me to be ready, occasionally wiping my lips with a damp cloth.

On one occasion I heard Evan's voice, just outside the door, roughly berating her for the amount of time she spent at my bedside, and refusing to move aside to let her pass along the corridor as she repeatedly asked, in a hushed but tearful voice. I tried to raise myself to go to her assistance, ashamed that a woman should be maltreated on my account, but immediately I felt such a stabbing pain in my neck and shoulder that I could go no further. I was relieved, however, to hear Llwys's voice, quietly insisting that there must be no further ado, and after that a silence fell back upon the house. I lay for some time, concentrating only on the pain I felt, until it lessened gradually, and once again I lost myself in the arm's of sleep.

The dreams seemed to occupy nine tenths of my life. Fantastical and tumultuous images surged through my mind like water over rapids, water through caves, down tunnels, swirling around culverts and other dark recesses. As is often the case with dreams, all preciseness seemed to be lost within moments of waking, leaving everything hidden behind a thick veil, but always, as I came back to myself, I found myself lying peacefully on a stretch of dry turf, and I could feel the rough grass in my hands, gripping it and feeling safe, like a ship in its moorings before I awoke fully to find myself in bed.

On the morning after I heard the argument with Evan, as I came out of my dreams, I felt, as usual, the dry turf under my body and the tufted grass in my hands. I turned my head, and Bryony was there, walking away down the sloping path of a hillside towards the sea, and as I lifted my head to look up, she turned and smiled, and at this point I opened my eyes and found myself alone in the room.

I managed to sit up and lift my legs out of the bed. My shoulder was stiff and sore but there was no repetition of the sharp and disabling pain I had felt the previous evening. I worked it round in a slow circle to ease the muscle, and for the first time since I had been brought from the wreck of the *Norman Court*, I felt that I was going to be well again.

With the assistance of the bedside chair, I lifted myself up, and managed to take three or four steps to the window, and pushing the curtain aside, looked out towards the shore, misty in the paleness of dawn.

I had been there for some time when Bryony came into the room.

"What are you doing?" she said, coming to my side.

She helped me back towards the bed. It was as well for already my strength was failing and I don't think I could have made it back alone.

"You're not ready for that yet," she said. "But you're getting better. The bruising on your shoulder is much improved. You have to build up your strength."

I told her about the strange dream, about waking up on the turf, though not that I had seen her in the dream.

"Perhaps you're remembering the day when you were brought here," Bryony said.

"Were you there?" I asked.

"The whole village was. There was nothing we could do to begin with, the weather was so wild. Then the Holyhead men came and they started to bring people to shore. You were put on the sward at the head of the beach, along with some others. They said you were dead at first, but your friend had them bring brandy and that made you splutter, and then they knew you were still alive."

"That would be Paolo," I said, remembering the fragmentary image I had of being untied from the red bandanna. "Are there any others still here?"

She shook her head. "Two were dead. They took them to Holyhead. Your friend stayed at the inn until the doctor said you were out of danger. The others went as soon as they had dry clothes."

I nodded. The pieces of what had happened were beginning to come together.

She made herself busy in the room, as if she thought it improper that she should stop work to chatter.

I had other questions I wanted to ask, but my eyes were closing again, and I seemed to drift into a thin sleep. I was aware, for part of the time at least, of her being in the room, though when I awoke fully once more, she was gone.

Chapter 4

My progress continued. I was soon able to walk unaided around the room, and for diversion would sit by the window, watching the changing sky and the breakers which made their way between the extensive rock flats, jagged and black, lying on each side of the bay. Before another week had passed, as the strength began to return to my legs, I was able, with assistance, to tackle the staircase, and spent many hours sitting in the garden at the side of the house. It was a sheltered spot, surrounded by a tall hedgerow which kept off the wind, and as the season changed to spring, it was a pleasant place to be alone with my own thoughts.

Free of the indignity of being fed by another hand, my appetite improved, and as a result of taking regular exercise, my tiredness was wholesome rather than enforced. Consequently my sleep became smoother and more refreshing. The doctor said that in two or three weeks more, I would be ready to begin the journey back to my home in Dublin.

That prospect in itself was a cause of mixed emotions. No-one recovering from a grave illness will deny the fillip to the spirits which comes with a physician's confident assertion that a full recovery is expected. The removal of the last vestiges of dependence, the ability to resume one's freedom – these are things which are greatly welcome. On the other hand, I knew that I could expect little in the way of indulgence from my father; that my return would no doubt prompt whatever he had in mind for the next stage of my preparation to enter the world of commerce, and I had a suspicion that that would involve a lengthy stint in the processing factories of northern England. At the same time, I had to acknowledge, privately at least, my sadness at the thought of severing the attachments I had made in my short time at Rhosneigr.

I should perhaps have mentioned that my personal ambition – one which I had cherished since my mother took me to exhibitions of art work in London on a trip there when I was twelve – was to train as an artist, but it was an aspiration which my father resolutely opposed.

The terrain in these parts makes it a perfect haven for those who would go in search of the beauties of nature and stimulation for the imagination. The immediate hinterland of Rhosneigr is low-lying, and a short way from the village lies the lake known as Llyn Maelog. This provides a supply of fresh water to the village, and became, in the final decades of the last century a centre of ship building, though nothing remains now of that industry. Instead the reed beds of the lake are busy with all kinds of birdlife, herons, snipes, reed warblers and many more. It is a place where unbroken peacefulness may be enjoyed.

In the near distance can be seen the bold headland of Holyhead mountain, and, further, on a clear day, the outcrops of the northern part of the island, Bodafon and Parys Mountain, whilst the perspective along the coastline includes the peaks of the Welsh mountain range, sometimes shrouded in cloud, sometimes startling in the clarity of its ridges and ravines, even from a distance of ten or twenty miles.

Along the sand dunes, on each side of the village, are the dwellings of fishermen, many of them little more than shacks, and their boats line the shore. The bay is bounded, on its northern side by the cliffs of Rhoscolyn, but the entire perspective is dominated by the plateaus of jagged rock, which become islands and submerged banks when the tide is full, and, since the day of my arrival, by the broken shell of the *Norman Court*.

Chapter 5

One morning, during the period when I was beginning to enjoy my new-found freedom of movement, I walked into the village, and spent half an hour chatting to the owner of the general store, Mr Hughes, who was also, as he told me, the organist at the church. He liked to boast that his store was the finest emporium on the island, stocking every commodity needful to the households of the parish, and, he added, much more besides. It was, I had to agree, a kind of Aladdin's cave, with several rooms reaching back into the depths of the building, packed with domestic necessities, sacks of beans, pulses, and cereals, hams and sides of bacon, as well as all manner of ingenious implements and curiosities. There was, besides, an intriguing and alluring trail of smells, coffee, smoked cheese, cured meats, spices, soap, paraffin, oil. On a cluttered shelf in one of the furthest rooms, there was a box of charcoal pencils and another of pastel crayons. Ordered, he explained, for a somewhat eccentric lady of the village, who had not kept the appointment to pick them up, and who, more latterly, had a more important appointment to keep, that is, with her maker.

"I'll take them," I said, on the whim of the moment.

"You'll be needing paper, then, too," he said, with the natural enthusiasm of the entrepreneur, as he led me across the room, and produced, from another shelf, an artist's sketchbook.

"Marbled cover boards and black calf," he said, holding it up for my inspection. "Beautifully bound, and just feel the texture of the paper, creamy, like vellum, that's what I would call it. Top quality vellum."

I went back to the house, with my new possessions, and, somewhat bashfully, that afternoon, announced my intention to do some sketching by Llyn Maelog.

My hand was clumsy at first, but I soon found a way to use simple lines and shading to represent the contours of the land, and by blending the pastel shades with my finger, it was possible to add touches of colour to the sky and the lake, the hills and the sea which captured a little of their quality and of their changing moods. They were passable, little more than that, I suspect, but the pleasure was largely in the fact of doing them, the concentration, the driving away of all other thought to the perimeter of consciousness, the knowledge gained by studying a scene and analysing closely the elements of its composition and structure.

Going further afield, I wandered along the cliff-top, one day, finding, in the direction of the mainland, the richest and most vivid array of perspectives including the headlands, the stretches of wide shore and sea, and the distant mountains. It was a set of land and seascapes which might have kept a professional artist busy for months, even years. I came at last to a wide estuary, with miles of sand, and following the stream inland, found myself in the quiet village of Aberffraw. I took a little refreshment at an inn there, and then, deciding that the cliff path might prove a little strenuous on my return, I made my way further inland, and before too long came to the embankment of the railway, which I followed back to Rhosneigr.

As we grew more familiar in each other's presence, I spoke to Bryony about my aspirations as an artist; she listened attentively but expressed no opinion; although her father was a man of books, there was no sign that she was aware of any greater world than that which surrounded the quiet village life which was her lot. Evan, on the other hand, getting word of it, made it the matter of jibes and mockery whenever he had the chance.

Chapter 6

Every morning, Llwys Llewellyn would stand for a while by the shore, looking out to sea, sometimes for twenty minutes, sometimes longer, completely still, scanning the horizon.

"We look to the sea in expectation," he said.

He told me of his eldest son, Bryn, who went to sea and never returned. "But even now, when I look out to the sea," he said, "I find a small place of hope in my breast."

He was also a keeper of bees. There was a small enclosed paddock, just across the lane from his garden, where he kept a dozen hives. On two or three occasions, I watched him as he tended the hives, pulling out the thick honeycombs for inspection, oblivious to the heavy swarming buzz around him. "In the study of bees," he told me, "we see God's hand in the complex interdependence of nature. Without the humble bee," he said, "much of the land would be bare of growth; they work tirelessly for their queen, but in their tireless labours they do untold service to mankind."

He also spoke, though with a heavy heart, of his sister. "She was a simple girl, good-hearted and too willing to believe goodness in others. She was abandoned, and only she believed that her seducer would return to keep his philanderer's promises. She died in childbirth, and so was spared the shame she had brought on herself. Evan was brought up with love around him, but a child, especially a boy, needs a proper father-figure, not one whose hair was white even before he was born."

It was during one of our conversations, after I had started sketching around Llyn Maelog, that Llwys told me of the shipbuilding that had once thrived in the locality. "It had mainly disappeared by the time I was a child," he said. "Just a few ruined buildings, and hoisting equipment fallen into decay. The boats were changing, you see, getting bigger, and they were sheathing the hulls with copper. The yard at Amlwch, with the deep water, took over, and thrived, though they say, now, that times are changing again, and even Amlwch will be left behind."

One morning, after I had been in Rhosneigr for five weeks, I received a letter from my father. It was not unkind but there was an unmistakable urgency in his wishes for me to return. It enclosed a banker's letter which I could encash in Holyhead. That afternoon, as I sat by Llyn Maelog, the peacefulness and tranquillity I felt were intensified all the more through my realisation of how quickly the time was approaching when I would have to leave.

That was the day when the first mysterious event took place.

Chapter 7

As I have said my sleep became much more regular, my dreams less disturbed now as each day passed by, but still, just in that strange and ill-defined interim between sleep and waking, I continued to experience the sensation that I was lying on a stretch of turf, gripping the rough grass with my hands, as if in fear that I would fall, into water or into space, before becoming aware, gratefully of the massive and reassuring solidity and of the earth beneath me.

As I awoke on this particular morning – I say morning though to judge from the light it was still some two or three hours before dawn – the usual sense of well-being I was accustomed to feel at waking in the knowledge of being safe, was absent. I gripped the coarse grass, as usual, anticipating the transition from sleep to waking and the disappearance of the illusion, but instead of finding myself in the warmth of my bed, I was aware of being chilled, and when I tried to pull the blanket around me, no blanket was there, only bare earth and rough grass.

I sat up suddenly, startled, and stared into the darkness, alert in every nerve, and listening to each sound like a hunted creature. What I heard was a disturbance of water, not the sound of a crashing surf, but that of the surface of water being whipped by sharp gusts of wind. As my eyes adjusted, and as the darkness resolved itself, I recognised the contours of the land in front of me as those of the lake, and that my own position was just a few feet away from the place where I had been sketching just a day or two before. I continued listening to ascertain the presence or otherwise of any other person, and became aware now of the sound of a metallic clinking in the high wind. Looking towards the far side of the lake, on the seaward side, I could see the faint tracery of masts and rigging reminiscent of boats gathered together in a small harbour, rolling and bobbing with the swell.

I picked myself up from the ground, expecting the usual twinge in my shoulder, the residual pain of my injury on the

Norman Court, but instead, strangely – though no more strange than everything else I was discovering – the movement of my shoulder was as free and easy as it had ever been. Following the path, now familiar enough, even in the darkness, I made my way around the edge of the lake. As I drew close I saw that the masts were those of boats in construction, surrounded by the apparatus of ladders and putlock platforms. I stood for a moment to verify the strange scene; closer inspection showed that it was no apparition or trick of the light. There was even a bench with two pewter tankards on it, and a canvas bag with a workman's tools, as if this was how it had been left at the end of the previous day's work.

It was impossible, I thought, that I could have missed seeing this corner of the lake during the days I had spent there, yet at the same time I told myself that it was too real, too solid to be the stuff of a dream.

My next instinct was to go to Llwys' house and bring someone to witness the scene, to gain some confirmation that it wasn't just a mental aberration, a lapse into madness, and so I set off on the short walk that linked the lake to the village.

I was within fifty yards or so of the village centre when I was overtaken by a young lad running down towards the shore.

"It's a ship on the rocks," he shouted, calling back to me.

I followed him down the hill and drawing closer, saw groups of storm lanterns, held aloft from clusters of shadowed people on the shore. The wind, coming now fully on from the open sea, was a constant gale, tugging and gusting at my clothes. The surf was thrashing onto the foreshore with a deep thunderous boom, and beyond, just visible in a sickly glimmering light, was surging over the Crygill rocks, sending sudden eruptions of angry foam high into the air.

At first I could see no evidence to support the boy's assertion that a boat was on the rocks. I made my way through the lanterns on the upper shore, held aloft mainly, it seemed, by older men, and women who tried to keep children back from the dangers of the surf. In the water itself, a dozen or so men were striving against the waves, their arms aloft as they tried to keep their balance, sometimes up to their shoulders and sometimes to their waists, as the tide roared forward and then dragged back.

It was at this point, as I calculated the direction of their striving, that my eye picked out the shadowy outline, fifty yards distant, of a boat in trouble on the shelf of rock which Llwys had told me was named Feurig Island.

Paolo had once entertained me with a story in which a marooned sailor, without food or water for nine days, had found himself looking down tranquilly on his own plight, as if his spirit, already released from his body, was bidding farewell as it took its leave. I wondered for a moment, if I was now, as it were, a ghost, witnessing the circumstances of the disaster which had brought about my own death, as the people on the shore stood watching, helpless spectators.

However, there was nothing tranquil or ethereal about what I was now observing: the men in the sea, shouting and cursing, the women on the shore, dragging back their children, who, fearless of danger, would join in the adventure – it was all too present, all too real.

Three men together, two who had been in the surf, and one who had gone forward to meet them, now dragged ashore a wooden chest which they had retrieved from the stormy water; almost immediately, half a dozen others joined them, and, like ants, they used their combined strength and effort to carry their burden towards the village.

At almost the same time, another group, just feet away, pulled a body from the water, and dragged it as far as they could onto the dry sand. It was a boy, no more than twelve, an apprentice or cabin boy, and from the reactions of those who tended to him, it was obvious, after a few moments, that he was beyond hope. They summoned others, and together they carried him, just as they must have done with me, to the dry turf at the head of the beach. Amongst those who carried him,

I recognised, even with her cloak and hood around her, the figure of Bryony.

I looked back towards the sea. The dawn light was now breaking from the landward, throwing a pale light on the breaking waves, sufficient to show an assortment of objects in the sea, and I heard someone say that because the ship was being broken on the rocks, the master was releasing the cargo, no doubt to see what could be retrieved to offset a total loss.

Emboldened by the prospect of salvage, the men in the surf now redoubled their efforts to be the first to lay claim to whatever they could grasp, and they were joined by others so that whole of the inner water seemed full of people competing like fish in a shoal.

Beyond them now, I could just make out the outline of two figures, struggling in the swell towards the shore. I don't believe the water was particularly deep, but the violent action of the surge made it almost impossible for them to keep their feet, and time and again, their heads disappeared under the water, only to reappear with desperate thrashing of arms and hands, several feet away from where they had previously been seen.

"It's a woman!" someone shouted.

I was myself in the water up to my waist by now, and like everyone else I turned my attention to the figure indicated by the caller, to see that it was indeed a female form, still some thirty feet away, and seemingly at the point of exhaustion. A group of men now strove towards her. Amongst them I recognised Evan, and despite the enmity between us, I admired his courage at that moment, for though I was standing in the surf, in truth, I dared go no further.

Feeling assured now of the woman's rescue, I looked for the other figure, but where he had been there was now no sign, and though I stared for several minutes together, it seemed that his struggle was over. He was found later, a hundred yards further along the beach where the tide had carried him.

With the tide now at the full, it was clear to see, as the weak morning light began to thin out the darkness, that the ship was nearly done. With the hull snapped, the relentless waves seemed to find every weakness, reducing her to a chaos of splintered timbers and floating wreckage, though even now, yet one more figure was visible, struggling across the reef towards the waters of the bay.

The group of men had now reached the hapless woman, and had drawn her into the shallower water, and yet, rather than bring her further to the safety of the shore, it seemed that they were searching about her pockets and clothing as if to find any valuables, money or jewellery that might be about her. There was some squabbling between them, and others were shouting angrily from the shore, though whether in protest at this treatment, or that they were being denied their proper share of the spoils, I know not. It was then, as I stared on shock and disbelief, that I saw a hand pushing the woman's head down, and holding it beneath the water. The hand belonged to Evan.

It was over so quickly that almost immediately I began to doubt the evidence of my own eyes. There were so many of them there, their hands flailing in the mad confusion of the water. Could I be certain that it was Evan's hand that had, so mercilessly, forced the woman's head down so that she must drown? Could I be certain that the action was as I had seen it and not an attempt at rescue that I had misconstrued? Or was there no such thing at all, only the desperation of men caught in extreme circumstances with their own lives hanging on a thread?

I backed off, out of the water, feeling faint, and recalling my own ordeal of just a few weeks before, sat down on the sand with my head on my knees, waiting for the dizzying wave of nausea to pass. When I was again sufficiently in possession of myself to take note of what was going on around me, I realised that a sharp stinging rain had now been added to the assault of the elements, and that I was shivering so violently that I could not even control the chattering of my own teeth.

The next thing I knew, a man was calling out, hoarsely, trying to make his voice heard above the wind by those who were still on the shore.

"For the love of God!" he shouted, "I am the master of the *Charming Jenny*, the sloop you have seen broken on the rocks here this day. Your people have taken the remnants of my cargo, whether for safekeeping or plunder, I know not, nor do I much care. But I saw my wife, struggling with the sea, and I believe she came safely to the shore. But I see her not now. For pity's sake, will no-one tell me where she is?"

He was led towards the head of the beach, and I, notwithstanding my own condition, summoned the resolve to follow, appalled at what I knew he must find there, and yet driven by some terrible fascination.

His wife was laid out on some sail cloth, as if that courtesy of keeping her from the ground might add some shred of dignity to her plight. Her face was a ghastly white, her lips the same. Someone had weighted her eyes long enough to hold them shut, perhaps otherwise fearing what a devilish tale those eyes open, even in death, might tell.

"There was nothing we could do for her."

"I told her to go, before it got worse. I helped her into the water. It seemed only a few feet … I thought…"

"Maybe you should have gone with her," said a voice, clinical in judgement.

"It was our fortune, everything we had…"

There was silence around, though the air was pregnant with the accusation that he had abandoned his wife and stayed to rescue his wealth.

The poor man screwed his face in anguish, suppressed a howl in his throat, and held her cold hand to his cheek. And then, suddenly, in horror, he expostulated, "What man has done this! What beast…" he faltered out, lost for words.

I looked at his dreadful staring eyes, fixed on the fourth finger of his wife's left hand, which he held tenderly in his own. The finger drooped slackly as if the bone had been snapped, deliberately snapped to make possible the removal of rings.

"I will have justice for this abomination," he shouted. "Let them know, every man in this village, that I will pursue them through hell, but I will have justice!"

He was persuaded, eventually, by the rector who by now was on the scene, and by two kindly souls who stayed by to calm him, that he must let his wife's body be carried away to be washed and laid out; he followed mumbling, almost out of his wits between self-recrimination and threats of bringing the full might of the law to bear.

Feeling a great weight of fatigue now on me, I decided it was time for me to return to Llwys' house, though I had no idea what I would say to them: would I dare broach with Evan the dreadful image I still had in my mind – for it had now returned with almost razor-like sharpness – of his forcefully immersing the poor woman's head, or mention it to Bryony who I knew had been there on the beach, too, and who might well have witnessed the same thing herself?

When I started to make my way, however, I found myself in a quandary, because, though I recognised the general layout of the village, none of the buildings I saw were as I remembered them, and the lane which led to Llwys's dwelling was no more than a grassy track which led to a few huts belonging, as I guessed, to the fishermen.

Confused, I turned back to follow the way I had come from the lake, an hour or two before, thinking I must have mistaken the point along the beach where I had emerged, but confident that if I could get back to the lake I would be able to find my way home from there.

As I crossed the narrow strip of land from the edge of the village to the lake, I noticed that the wind had now dropped, and that instead of rain, a mist was now slowly creeping in from the sea. As I passed the ship-yard, three or four men were now beginning their day's work. I called a greeting to them, but they did not reply. I stood to watch them for a moment, climbing ladders up onto the putlock, but the mist was thickening, and I wondered if they would be forced to stop working if it worsened any further. Feeling the pain in my shoulder, which had resumed – at first almost without my noticing it – growing worse, I hurried on, but after a few minutes, as I reached the point from where I had done my sketching, it became so severe that I was forced to sit down and take a rest.

When I looked back along the side of the lake, the mist had gone completely, leaving now what seemed the beginnings of a pleasantly blue hazy dawn. The shipyard itself, and everything surrounding it, the ladders and hoists, the masts and platforms, the men at work, all had vanished completely.

Too tired now to question this, and cradling my aching shoulder, I hurried on. A kind of numbness now came over my mind, and when I came to the lane leading to Llwys' house, and recognised the hedge at the front of his garden, I felt a great sense of relief. There was a sound of business in the kitchen, but otherwise there was no stirring in the house. I made my way as quietly as I could up to my chamber, and, wrapping myself in a great-coat, sat down in the chair by the window and almost immediately, fell asleep.

Chapter 8

"You look tired," said Bryony, bringing a ewer of hot water to my room as she did each morning. "Did you not sleep well?"

"It's just my shoulder. It was hurting in the night, so I got up."

"I'll bring the doctor."

"No, it's all right," I protested. "It's nothing."

"It's better if he has a look at it," she retorted, firmly.

She left the room, and I wondered that there was not the least flicker of recognition in her eye at what we had both witnessed just a few hours before.

I poured some water into the bowl and washed my hands and face, then changed into some fresh clothes, though in fact the clothes I took off bore no evidence, as I had supposed, of the ill-use they had been subjected to at the edge of the sea earlier that day.

A few minutes later, I heard the doctor's footsteps on the stair. He sat me down on the side of the bed, and pulled back my shirt.

"The bruising's less, in fact," he said considerately, moving my shoulder around. "Feel any more pain now?"

"Not especially."

He nodded and hummed. "Probably just the way you lay on it. I'll ask Bryony to see you get more pillows. Can't have you missing your sleep."

Sleep, I reflected, after he had left - had I had any sleep at all, or was the whole experience the product of sleep?

I managed to eat a little breakfast, and then walked down to the shore. It was now a pleasant morning, with the sun breaking through thin cloud, and the lightest of breezes from the south. In the middle of Cremlyn Bay, towards Rhoscolyn, the *Norman Court*, or what remained of her, was sitting on the reef where she had foundered, a gentle swell playing idly over the broken ribs and spars. I stood exactly where I had been when they dragged the dead woman out of the sea; there was no evidence of any other wreck, or of the disturbance I had witnessed, though I could recall every detail, even to the point where Evan's hand had pushed the woman's head under the water. That, more than anything else had the starkness of reality.

You may be forgiven for thinking a man suffering from a recent blow to the head, and given to dreaming, may be an unreliable witness in such a tale as the one I have just presented. Believe me, I have thought so myself and questioned myself, for many hours together, as rigorously as one in the dock.

I know that dreams often reflect those things which preoccupy or trouble us most, frequently in a distorted, magnified or grotesque way. This had happened to me in the East Indies, waking up at odd hours through the night, bathed in sweat, slipping in and out of dreams, and picturing things I had seen during the day, a man and horse dead in a mudslide, a child, its stumps of arms dusted with the white of leprosy, a blind beggar in Jacarta, his empty eye sockets bearing the evidence of knife scars.

In the present circumstances, there was an obvious pattern: a recent shipwreck in which I had, myself, come close to drowning, villagers on the shoreline, as Bryony had described them, assisting the rescue. And as for Evan, and the fact that I had seen him perpetrate a dreadful crime, might that not reflect some deep antipathy I felt towards him for his obvious resentment of my presence as an invalid in the house?

There was also the business of the shipyard to consider. Certainly I had never seen that shipyard, but I had been told of its existence, and during the sessions I had spent sketching by the lake, I had speculated as to where it might have been and what it might have looked like. It was quite within reason to suppose that my own imaginings had left a sufficient impression to become part of the imagery of a dream.

Had it not been for certain factors which would not allow me easily to reach the obvious conclusion, I would have been quite prepared to concede that the whole experience belonged within the provenance of dreaming. To begin with dreams are characteristically only flimsily coherent – definition shifts and slides, distinctions dissolve, images and sequences modulate and undergo transitions which owe nothing to the orderly logic of everyday life. I have also noted that most dreams vanish on waking; even dreams which are vivid at the moment of waking will disappear like breath from a mirror within moments, leaving the faintest hint of what they were. What I had experienced had none of this fluidity; it was as vivid and cogent as my memory of yesterday or the day before.

I have also noticed, occasionally, that there are stages when the dream-state and the knowledge of its being a dream overlap for an infinitesimal moment. *This is only a dream,* you say to yourself, sometimes in relief, sometimes wistfully, as the apparatus of the dream recedes. In my experience of the previous night, there had been no such transition; indeed, even whilst it was taking place, I had been able to say to myself, *this is strange, but it is not a dream, it is real.*

I tried also to consult such knowledge as I had of illusory experiences caused by the use of narcotics. I recall that the poet, Coleridge, in composing his famous piece *Kublai Khan*, claimed that the whole poem came to him in a waking vision, and that when that vision was interrupted by the arrival to the house of a visitor, he was quite unable to recreate it, leaving the poem as the merest fragment of what it might have been. In the East Indies I had, on three or four occasions, savoured the pleasures of the opium pipe and in those poppy states of mind had experienced the strange unreal pleasure streams accompanied by waking dreams that come from the influence of that strange plant, though looking at those poor human wrecks who had become its slave was quite sufficient to persuade me against anything other than the most occasional indulgence.

During my conversation with the doctor, that morning, he confirmed, in response to a question I had put to him, that he had administered laudanum when my pain was at its height but added that he had not done so for over a week, and that he very much doubted that any trace of that preparation could still be active in my system.

I was left to conclude that what had happened was neither a natural dream, nor a hallucination precipitated by external means, chemical or herbal. With these certainties, and faced with the uncomfortable proposition that only a madman believes things to have happened which no-one else in the world can corroborate, nothing would have dissuaded me from believing myself to have suffered some kind of waking delusion of madness, had I not decided to speak to Llwys, and to put some questions to him on that which I believed myself to have seen.

Chapter 9

From the earliest days of my recovery, as soon as I was well enough to have company, it had been Llwys' habit to spend a little time with me each day, and though at that stage it was difficult for me to sustain a full part in the conversation, it was pleasant enough to hear him talk. His voice was low and quiet, and it had a soothing and reassuring effect on me at a time when I was still prone to bouts of panic and alarm. Later, when I was able to move around and sit outside, we would often spend an hour or so in each other's company, sometimes, as I have said, tending the beehives, or sitting in the garden, or taking a stroll to the corner of the village or the margin of the sea. The conversation was always easy and natural; sometimes he would ask me about the sugar trade, or my father's business in Dublin; sometimes he would tell me about the village and its people. Often enough, we would sit or walk in silence, and there was never a sense of awkwardness; indeed, in those easy thoughtful silences, I felt completely at one with myself and with the world.

After my exploration of the beach that morning, I returned to the cottage, and sitting by the window in my room, dozed for an hour. For the rest of the afternoon, still tired, I kept to my room, and then joined the family for their meal in the early evening. Later, seeing Llwys in the garden below I went down to join him. He raised his hand in acknowledgment, and I took my place on the bench by his side.

"A beautiful day," he said, with an open gesture of his hand towards the sky, still rosy with dusk. "Our Anglesey weather is not always so clement, though you know Anglesey is also known as Mam Cymri, the mother of Wales, so called because in ancient times, the fertility of the land surpassed that of all other regions."

I nodded and smiled.

"You walked by the shore earlier today," he said. "I hope it doesn't bring unpleasant memories."

For a moment, I was tempted to confide the entire story to him, but thought better of it. However, it was not difficult to divert the conversation in the direction I wished.

"I suppose a great many ships must have been wrecked in these waters," I began. He nodded slowly, reflectively and then, at his own pace, took up the tale.

"I dare say there are places in the world where harsher seas meet more fearsome shores than here," he began, "but let them tell their own tale. There's not a length of coast, from here to Amlwch, on the north of the island, and to Beaumaris and Porthaethwy in the east, where the sea-bed isn't strewn with broken ships, and where the winds haven't carried the forlorn prayers or desperate screams of men about to drown."

His own son, Bryn, he told me, had been lost in a full tempest when his fishing smack was thrown onto the rocks of the Skerries. Three of a seven man crew, clinging onto loose timbers, managed to scramble back to the shore, half dead, to tell the tale. The rest perished. He himself had gone to Holyhead to see the Great Eastern at anchor there on the night of the great storm of 1859, and had seen ships going down even in the shelter of the new breakwater. "That was the night, of course," he went on, "when *the Royal Charter* was broken on the rocks at Moelfre, and the people there weren't so much drowned as battered on the jagged rocks."

"There was a ship I heard of once," I ventured, trying to make it seem like a distant half-memory, "that was lost somewhere near here, on the rocks, the *Jenny something*, or the *Cheerful Jenny*…"

"The *Charming Jenny*" he corrected immediately, and though I tried to let no sign of it slip, my excitement could not have been greater at the corroboration of what, outside my 'dream', I had no possible means of knowing

He shook his head slowly, and twisted his lip in an awkward grimace, so that for some time I did not know whether he would continue or whether the reference to the ship was going to lead to nothing more than a long thoughtful silence.

"It's over a hundred years ago," he continued at last, "and what exactly happened on that night, no one knows. Even my grandfather, who was there, and who told me the tale, could not say for certain - unless he was protecting me from the worst of it, as has sometimes occurred to me - but by his account it was a bitter September night. He was only a boy himself at the time, no more than eight or nine, and as likely as not he was bemused by all that was going on."

Although I was still staggering at the revelation that the event which I seemed to have witnessed concurred with something that had taken place so long ago, I found myself wondering if Llwys's grandfather might have been one of those youngsters I had seen amongst the crowds on the beach, when those terrible events were taking place.

"He used to tell me tales of wrecking," Llwys went on, "just to get me off to sleep at night, and I know now that there was more imagination in it than truth, and I loved the exaggeration for he included sea monsters and all manner of things that thrilled me to sleep – but on that particular story, there was always a different manner, a solemnity – and I knew that though he may not have known everything, he was making none of it up."

He paused, looking towards the house, and I saw that Bryony had just come from the kitchen door with a tray of tea. She set it down on the table before us, and poured a cup for each of us. Llwys smiled and squeezed her hand, and I thanked her, too, though catching her eye, I detected a faint unease, as if she felt some apprehension at what might be the subject of our conversation.

Llwys took two or three sips of the hot tea, replaced his cup in the saucer, and then continued with his tale. "Of course," he said, "there were always rumours of false lights."

"False lights?" I asked.

"Lights set up to deceive ships out at sea," he explained. "To lure them onto the rocks and then set about plunder."

He raised his hand at the look of horror on my face. "I called them rumours," he explained. "And so I believe them to be. No more than that, for there's nothing people like more than a lurid tale when they sit around their fires at night, or around a tavern bench when the drink is flowing. I've lived here now above seventy years and I've heard tales of fairies and hobgoblins but I've never seen one! Nor have I ever come across a shred of evidence that that any ship was deliberately wrecked.

"But certainly, the story of the *Charming Jenny* is one which casts a shadow on our history. The master's wife died, you understand, and a man and boy who were all the crew. Only the master survived, Captain Chilcott, and he made it his business to have recourse to the law. His wife had come ashore with her jewellery, they said, and a purse of sovereigns, and it was all gone, even the silver buckles from her shoes had been ripped off. Half a dozen were arraigned for theft of spirits and other goods from the wreck. One man, Sion Parry was convicted at Shrewsbury, and hanged, and his family moved away to Amlwch for the shame of it. The Crygill robbers they called them, and that name stuck, so there you are."

He shook his head a little sadly and sipped the last dregs of his tea. For my part, the details he had revealed, confirming so much of what I had witnessed with my own eyes, sent a chill through my very being.

"But another thing that's true," he said, resuming, "and I have witnessed examples of this many times, all through my life, in fact, is this: folk who live close by the sea look on the sea as a provider and I don't just mean the fish! You see the main beam of my house and the lintel over my door – all from the sea, ship's timbers washed up on the shore or plucked from the sea. Rolls of cloth, barrels of liquor, rope, candles, tools and implements, even crockery have been known to come ashore with no crime committed to bring it there, and you see, people see that as providence."

"I imagine the Receiver of Wrecks might have something to say about that!" I ventured, attempting a lighter vein.

Llwys cackled a little in his throat with mirth. "I've never yet seen a Receiver risk his own life going aboard a storm tossed ship to save others, but I've seen many men of the coast do just that. And if men are bold enough to retrieve that which would otherwise be lost to the sea, who is to say they don't have a claim to be the rightful owner?

"Of course, there was an old belief that if you save a life from the sea, you owe the sea a life, and that the sea will seek your own – call it just an old superstition, it terrifies some people. Yet I've never known a man of Rhosneigr or anywhere else hereabout go about plunder or salvage or wrecking, whatever you choose to call it, whilst there was still a life to be saved.

"Another factor is this - that people were poor, not poor as we think it now, but poor to the point of starvation, and isolated, too, - in my grandfather's day there were no proper roads even from one part of the island to another and it might be, saving your own exception, that men or women rescued from the sea had to be cared for from scant resources, maybe through a long winter of hard weather with just enough laid down to get by.

"Things are hard enough now, at times, and you've seen yourself that people of Rhosneigr don't set meat on their table every day of the week, but then there were no trains bringing in supplies, and when the harvest was poor..."

He finished at last and by this time the light had long faded and we both acknowledged that it was time for rest. As we went back into the house, I passed Bryony in the corridor from the kitchen, and I fancied, once again, that there was a look of questioning recognition in her eye.

Despite the events of the day, however, and the tangle of unanswered questions in my mind, I slept well that night, and it was a sleep all the more peaceful for being untroubled by a single dream.

Chapter 10

The following day saw the end of the fine weather. The wind changed to the east, so that even though the year had advanced beyond the flourishing and disappearance of the May blossom, the fires in the grates of Llwys' house were lit in the evenings to keep the chill from the air.

On the morning after my conversation with Llwys, I made my first visit to Holyhead, and with the papers my father had sent me, drew money from the bank. I made a tour of the harbour, observing the improvements which Llwys had described to me. The port and its facilities have expanded greatly since the acquisition of the Irish trade some sixty years ago, an expansion consolidated by the advent of the railway in the following decade. Now, there are seven sailings a day out of Holyhead to Ireland, two carrying mail, two passengers, two freight, all to the port of Kingstown, and a seventh to Greenore, on Carlingford Lough. A similar and corresponding number of inbound ships is catered for each day, so that the port and the town which serves it has an air of business about it to compare with any I have seen, saving Liverpool.

It had been my intention, as part of the business of the day, to make arrangements for my own homeward passage, but on that crucial matter, and against my father's express wishes, I made the decision to delay, and as soon as I returned to Rhosneigr that evening, I sought out Llwys and asked his permission to extend my stay by a week. He smiled and nodded courteously, and I truly believe he welcomed my wish to prolong my stay under his roof.

When I produced my pocket-book, however, and drew out notes, explaining that it was my intention to compensate for the expense I must have put on the household, he demurred.

"You are a guest in my house," he said. "Hospitality is the gift which God gives us so that we may give it to others. It enriches our own lives."

"You are truly the most gracious of hosts," I said, "but perhaps there are those in the house who would not see things in quite the same way."

"Money alone never made a true friend," he replied. "But to keep the peace, I will accept your offering as a gift, and will make sure your generosity is known."

At table that evening, Evan, who was characteristically sullen and uncommunicative on these occasions, asked me how my day had been, and though I sensed that this was from some prompting from Llwys, the concession was not unwelcome. Megan smiled archly at me. Bryony continued to eat her meal in silence.

The same evening, I wrote to my father, making excuses for a few days' delay. I told him I was still experiencing spells of faintness and dizziness, that I was not yet ready for a journey of any length, especially not a sea journey. There was some truth in this; but some disingenuity, too. There was, I sensed, with apprehension and excitement in equal measure, unfinished business for me in Rhosneigr. One aspect of this, though perhaps I did not fully understand it at the time, was that I was beginning to fall in love with Bryony.

Chapter 11

Dirty weather lingered with us for several days. The cold spell from the east was followed by persistent gusting south westerlies; ranks of cloud and columns of rain followed each other with monotonous regularity from the smudged sea horizon to the land, and the distant mountains wore a funereal shroud of mist. Save where the sun strove intermittently to penetrate the labyrinth of clouds, succeeding only in creating a silvery gleam, all the colours were in shades of grey.

Life in Rhosneigr continued with a certain grim acceptance of normality. There was work to be done, under a gloomy sky just as under a smiling heaven, fields to be tended, bedding and linen to be washed, floors to be swept, windows to be cleaned. The weather, except in extremes, made little difference to the fishermen, who put out each day with the morning tide, or at the blacksmith's forge where Evan toiled in the heat of the furnace each day.

In the evenings, we would sit in the parlour for an hour. Llwys would read – he had just acquired, I recall, a volume containing the works of Goronwy Owen whom he much admired – whilst I dabbled with my sketches, and Bryony and Megan worked at their needlepoint. Megan, sensitive of the proximity of so many in the room, including, no doubt, myself, was given to short bursts of shrill giggling, drawing admonition from Llwys for her lack of self-control, though I have to admit that her attempts to suppress laughter were more a source of amusement to me than annoyance. Bryony would give no reaction, but would continue to look down at her work with unbroken concentration, though I detected sometimes a faint colouring of embarrassment at her sister's frivolity. On one occasion, I ventured to begin a small sketch of her in the corner of another drawing I was trying to improve, and looking up, to confirm a detail of her brow, I found her eyes looking directly at mine. It was just for the briefest of moments, for she looked down again almost immediately, but even though my sketch was concealed from her eyes and from all others in the room except my own, I felt certain that she had guessed perfectly the business in which I was employed.

Evan did not join us on these occasions, but two or three times a week would take himself to the tavern where he played dominoes and cribbage with other fellows of the town. Llwys did not approve of his regular drinking, but Evan's characteristic retort was that it was not his fault if, after a long day over the forge, his throat was burning with thirst, and to this Llwys offered no counter-argument. To be fair to him, though he was by temperament given to blunt and unvarnished expressions of his opinions and feelings, I never knew Evan come home drunk.

Though I missed the summery evenings when we sat outside, Llwys and I, the tranquillity of those evenings in the parlour when we sat together with the weather drawn about the house, were a tonic to my spirits and I found myself daydreaming of how pleasant it would be to continue this way forever and never return home.

One evening, nearly a week after my visit to Holyhead, a wind had blow up outside, rattling the casement, and though we all concentrated on our tasks, even Megan, there was a sense of an unease which we shared but did not speak of; then, suddenly there was a gust of high wind which whistled violently around the eaves, and we all looked up together, momentarily torn from our private thoughts, united in sudden terror of what would happen next.

Part 2

The White Raven

Chapter 12

The girl knew he was following her, but he did not know whether or not she was afraid. As they entered the village, she quickened her pace, and it was difficult to keep track of her as she made her way through the clusters of dwellings. Only once she looked back, and their eyes met in recognition. Then she hurried on again, and when he came to the corner where she had turned just a moment before, she was entering the gate of a palisade surrounding more substantial buildings. He hurried across the cleared space in front of the palisade, but as he reached the gateway, the heavy oak doors, embossed with metal studs, were already closing, and a moment later, he heard the sound of the solid wooden bolts sliding into place.

A group of children who, he realised, had been following, now gathered around him curiously.

"Stranger!" called a man, with long grizzled hair, tied up behind, wearing a woollen tunic, a long goat-skin shoulder cloak and boots of tanned hide. At a signal from him, the children dispersed.

The younger man looked towards him. He smiled, showing a row of blackened and carious teeth, and then approached, using a wooden staff to support a pronounced limp on his left leg. There was nothing threatening in his demeanour, but the younger man knew he would have to find some way of explaining his presence.

"Have you travelled from far?" he asked.

"Just from the river below," he answered, which, in truth, was as much as he knew.

"You will be of Matholwch`s company, then?"

"Yes," he replied, glad to take hold of any straw that was offered.

The old man grinned even more widely, and then clapped him warmly on the shoulder. "Then welcome, indeed, and a stranger no longer. And thank God that your master has been pacified over Efnisian's rudeness, at last. Now we may look forward to some festivities."

"Let's hope so."

"Our Efnisian is a hot-head, there's no doubt about it, and his pride was injured, but he's a warrior first and foremost, and warriors sometimes act before they think. I should know, I was one myself for long enough."

"Is that how you gained your wound?"

He lifted his cloak and there was a long white scar across the ligaments behind his knee. "A strategic retreat," he grinned, but the devil was a fleeter of foot than me. Still, I managed to turn as I fell, and sliced his belly as he came in for the kill. He wasn't expecting that."

He laughed again, and then said, "Come with me, young fellow, you look as if you could do with some refreshment."

The young man followed as his new acquaintance led the way, talking constantly, obviously proud of his people and his village. His name, he said, was Garwyn, once Garwyn the Warrior, now Garwyn of the Limp, though he was keen to point out that the latter title was an honour and not a jibe. His Master, who he called King of Affalach, had rewarded him with many gifts, he said, and his deeds were still recorded in the songs of the Bards. "You'll hear it at the festivities," he said, and then added, with a chuckle in his voice, "you may have to listen carefully, mind you, or you might miss it, but it's there somewhere!"

He led a winding path through the huts which the young man had noticed before, when pursuing the girl. They were round in shape, with low walls of closely woven hazel, and roofs of thatch which came almost to the ground. They came, after five minutes or so, to a hut which was larger than the others and set slightly aside, with wicker hurdles to protect it from the wind on one side. Two dogs sat by the entrance, dogs which looked as if they might have been trained for hunting, though like Garwyn, it seemed that their triumphant days might well have been in the past. On a spit over a low fire, a skinned rabbit was cooking.

"This is my house," said Garwyn. "Come inside."

A square entrance, between sturdy posts cut directly from the halved trunk of a tree, and decorated with concentric circles, geometric patterns of lines and some animal forms, led to the inside of the hut. It was more spacious than might have been imagined, pleasantly cool and with dry rushes on the floor and strewing herbs that gave off a pleasing, fresh aroma. To one side, for there were several distinct areas within the dwelling, a young woman was sitting at a stool, manipulating the warp and weft of what was evidently a simple weaving frame.

"This is Ceri, my sister's son's daughter. She will serve us."

She was a comely girl, of fifteen or sixteen, with flowing brown hair, and a quick lively eye. "Well, go on girl!" he ordered. "Stop staring and get on with it."

"Yes, grandfather," she replied, the admonishment having little effect to diminish the pert smile on her lips.

"Her father serves the King directly, one of his chosen guards, as I once was, and therefore he lives in the Royal Compound. That's where you were when I came across you."

"Tell me," said the young man, feeling increasingly comfortable in the older man's affable company, "who is the woman who passed through the gate?"

"The one you were following?" said Garwyn, with another of his chuckles.

"I wasn't following her. Not exactly. Well, I saw her in the meadow down below, just by the river, and she reminded me of someone I know. I thought for a moment it was this person. I was mistaken, of course."

"Every man who catches sight of a beautiful woman would like to think he knows her!" said Garwyn, and he snorted loudly with laughter.

At this moment, Ceri returned. She carried a tray from which she set down an earthenware bowl filled with blackberries, two goblets and a jug. Then she poured some water into a larger bowl, and, kneeling, washed her grandfather's hands and then those of the young man.

"Look at her," said Garwyn. "She's fifteen and she's mad to find a husband. Watch out, young fellow, for I can see she's already practising a sweet look for you!"

"Stop it, grandfather," said the girl, colouring slightly. "Try to be as your age should guide you to be, gracious and wise, and not as a jester who would make the king laugh at the another's discomfort!"

Garwyn laughed all the louder at this remonstrance, and it was clear that he liked the girl's spirit. "She has a candle burning for Efnisian, but he's beyond her reach. Still, anyone may hope!"

"I've no flame for Efnisian," said the girl. "His temper is legendary. He's become an embarrassment to us all."

This, the young man observed, was the second reference to the man called Efnisian. He would have liked to ask for clarification, but felt that, in the guise he had adopted, it was something he would be assumed to know.

By now the girl had filled the two goblets from the jug, a golden cordial which had the scent of honey, and whose taste was sweet but with a hint of fire that could be felt, almost immediately, in the blood.

"You were about to tell me..." said the young man.

"Was I...? What?" said Garwyn, who was momentarily in a state of abstraction savouring his drink.

"The woman who entered the compound."

"Oh, yes, Well, that's Princess Branwen, daughter of Llyr and Penarddun, sister of Bran and Manawydan, and half-sister of Nisien and Efnisian, also known as white raven, who we partly worship as a Goddess. So, I'm sorry to disappoint you if you had any aspirations in that direction, but as you have already no doubt worked out yourself, she it is for whose hand in marriage your master Matholwch has come here as a suitor, she it is who, when you return with your fleet across the sea to Eirean, will be your new queen. So let's have another drink to celebrate this glad state of affairs. Ceri!"

The girl returned and dutifully filled the goblets. "Is there anything else, grandfather? Would you like some more blackberries?"

This satirical note – for not a single berry had been taken from the bowl – was lost on Garwyn, but the girl shared her joke, by means of a quick twinkling look of the eye, with their visitor.

"Yes, she's the girl your Matholwch has come to marry. Efnisian's half sister, you see. He took umbrage that the marriage was arranged without his consent. Though why it should matter so much to him, I don't know, unless, as some people say, he's in love with her himself."

"With his sister?"

Garwyn shrugged, giving the impression that he did not think this altogether unusual. "She's a beautiful girl, and a queen and a goddess. If Bran thought marriage between Efnisian and Branwen good for tribe, it would be so."

"Why Bran? Why not Llyr, her father? Didn't you say that Bran was her brother, too?"

"Bran is of the race of giants, as is Branwen," said Garwyn, seeming to think this a perfectly easy and satisfactory explanation.

"What does 'white raven' mean?"

"The raven is a goddess of war, though white also signifies Branwen's purity of soul, which means that she has the power to transport the spirits of the departed to the otherworld."

By the time the young man came out of Garwyn's dwelling, the light was already fading. Garwyn accompanied him part of the way back down the hill, to a vantage point where they could see the meadows and the river below. The grazing animals were now being led to the lower slopes of the village, where they were herded into pens. At the mouth of the estuary, a haze over the sea, suffused with late sunlight, softened the edges of the landscape. The young man turned, and set his steps in the direction of home.

Chapter 13

The above is my imperfect attempt, written immediately after the event – what I might term my second excursion through the curtain of time - to objectify what happened, by adopting the detached style of a third person narrative. But it doesn't help, only serving to falsify, and decorate with an artifice of superficial truth, that which cannot properly be explained.

I will, therefore, now revert to my journeyman's attempt to render the experience exactly as it seemed to happen at the time.

The girl of course was Bryony, but before I saw her and began to follow her, I had already walked for four or five miles, until I found myself on the shores of Llyn Coron, and there picked up the course of the river towards Aberffraw.

It started as before, gripping the turf beneath me for safety, only on this occasion, the over-riding sensation, to begin with at least, was that of being unable to breathe. I remember being told, as a child, that just as a man may drown in the sea, so a fish may drown in the air. What degree of scientific accuracy this has, I am unsure, it may simply be a childish analogy, but what I felt, for twenty or thirty seconds was that I was drowning in the air. It seemed, at first, that my lungs were striving to take in air that was dead, to extract from it life-sustaining properties that simply weren't there, perhaps like the air of an ancient tomb. Just at the point when I thought I must expire, however, the quality of the air modified into what seemed an intense green freshness, as rich as the other was sterile, and almost as difficult to breathe.

It was a good five minutes before my lungs felt free of the strain, and before my chest began to move steadily and easily again. It was only then that I was able to begin taking stock of my surroundings. It was night, but there was sufficient light, from a moon that was now waning over the sea, and from stars that occasionally shone through from behind a shifting muslin of clouds, to see that I was once again on the shore of

Llyn Maelog. Looking up, I feared that I would see the boatyard, as I had before, and would be forced to relive the whole of that nightmarish experience once more.

The broad sweep of the lake, however, was empty. I followed the path, as I had done before, to the narrow strip of land that separated the lake from the sea-shore, and then turned towards the village of Rhosneigr.

Reflected in the sea, the light was stronger here, revealing, in shadowy low outcrops, the rocks of Crigyll, Ynys Feurig and Cremlyn Bay, all swimming peacefully, it seemed, in a calm sea. A few small fishing boats were drawn up beyond the high water mark, and the sea, I judged, was some twenty minutes beyond the slack of a full tide. At the head of the beach stood a rough shelter of driftwood and woven sea-grass, but along the whole curving stretch of the bay, from Rhosneiger to Silver Bay and beyond to the low cliffs of Rhoscolyn, there was, apart from this, not a single building.

For some time, maybe ten minutes, maybe longer, I surveyed the desolate prospect, until I decided at last that nothing would happen without my taking some action myself, and for want of any better plan, I set my steps in the direction of Aberffraw. I soon decided, however, that I dared not trust myself to the coastal path which I had followed, in the full daylight, just a few days before my trip to Holyhead. The cliffs, though not high, were full of fissures where a man might easily stumble in the dark and break an ankle, and sudden turns and twists of the rock into narrow coves with sheer drops below. It was for this reason that I decided to follow the inland path.

Away from the coast, the darkness became more complete. The moon had now dropped beneath the rim of the horizon, and the cloud above had thickened, closing out the stars. In most places, even remote places, where I have been at night, there is always some incidental source of light, a village, a farmhouse on the hill, an individual dwelling by the wayside; but here there was nothing, just a velvety blackness like a canopy that had been draped all around.

The darkness contains terrors, both real and imaginary, for all but those with nerves of steel, and I do not pretend to be of that constitution. That which can be seen can be faced, that which lurks in the depth of the shadow remains a dreadful enigma: wild animals, brigands lying in wait to pounce and leave one for dead, beasts half-human half-devil – any hostile entity may be conceived by the lonely traveller along a darkened road at night.

Part of my difficulty, too, from a practical point of view, was that in my earlier return journey on foot from Aberffraw, I had followed the course of the railway; now, however, there was no railway to follow, only a rough track; and as the light began to dawn at last, I began to realise how much the land had been changed, for where now my way wound around the slopes and contours of rough heathland, I could picture deeply entrenched cuttings and embankments which allowed the railway track to be laid in a straight line and to an even gradient.

I came at last, with the sun rising over the hills to my left, to the hill above Llyn Coron, and made my way down to the bank. On the far side of the lake, I recognised the point at which the Ffraw began its course towards the sea, though from this vantage point, the prospect was almost entirely different. Instead of the little brook which wound its lazy way through meadows onto the wide sand flats below Aberffraw, the river dropped quickly into a wide tidal estuary. A mile distant, two dozen sea-going ships were moored, along with a score or more of fishing smacks, some of which were already setting out towards the sea. It had every sign of being a busy thoroughfare of sea-going traffic.

Where, on my earlier excursion, I had by-passed the sleepy village of Aberffraw, I now looked on the settlement where I was to be entertained by Garwyn and his sister's son's daughter, Ceri. It spread around the low hill in a series of concentric ramparts, the lowermost of the earthen mounds set about with a six foot wooden palisade. At the summit, and looking down over the settlement as a whole like a citadel, was visible the group of timber built halls and turrets into which I was shortly to see Bryony's figure disappearing.

Before I reached the harbour I came upon a pool by the side of the river where the stream water had been diverted to form a basin of fresh water. Here, a dozen girls were washing clothes, some with their sleeves rolled up, some stripped to the waist, their breasts exposed. At the sight of me, appearing suddenly, they screamed and giggled, and ran off out of sight. I took the opportunity to avail myself of a woollen smock, that was hanging to dry, and some strips of leather and cloth and rope, also laid out in the sun. Having retreated to a sheltered corner nearby, and divesting myself of my coat, I put on the smock, and wrapped the cloth and leather about my legs and feet in the way I had seen amongst some of primitives in East Timor. The rope, wrapped around my waist, completed my costume, enough, I hoped, to get by without attracting too much attention to myself.

Thus garbed, I moved on, and so it was, full of curiosity, observing the business of the harbour, and the activities of the surrounding meadows and the lower slopes, that I caught sight of Bryony passing through the gateway and beginning to make her way up towards the village. I sensed straight away that she had already seen me, and that that perhaps was the cause of her haste, and without thinking twice, I began to follow. I felt if I could make her acknowledge me once in this strange world, it would be the means of making her talk to me about it.

I was vaguely aware, as I followed her, of other activities that made up the business and organisation of the village: carts carrying grain up the hill, an enclosure where pigs were kept, animal pelts hanging to be cured on wooden frames, a fire and bellows worked by a boy, an apprentice, and the din of metal the smith worked at what looked like a plough. But I was too preoccupied with not losing sight of Bryony, to take in more detail than that, even to think that there might be any danger to myself in being a stranger in such a place.

Then she turned just once, as I've mentioned, and I felt sure, from the look in her eyes, that she knew me.

A moment later, she was gone, the gate was locked, and that was when I turned to see Garwyn.

My meeting with him was both a pleasure and a source of anxiety. The anxiety, of course, lay in the expectation that at any moment, I would say something to invalidate the thin disguise he had helped me to assume, the identity of a sailor of a visiting and more or less friendly neighbouring kingdom. On the whole, however, I think he was simply glad of company, and besides the conversation I have already recorded, there were numerous tales and digressions that filled the passage of several hours. In addition to his goodwill and simple hospitality, there was also, if I am to record my impressions fully, the charm and good-humour of Ceri, his sister's son's daughter, who called him grandfather – though I think that term was meant to describe an older kinsman rather than any precise relationship. As far I could tell, notions of family, and kinship and tribe ran into each other with a blurring of distinctions which caused them no difficulty at all.

The conversations I have recorded are, I have to admit, approximate. One tries, obviously, to give a version which is sufficiently fluent for a reader to follow, but in fact our exchanges were a good deal more halting than might appear to be the case, requiring much repetition, choice of alternative words, hand gestures, pointing and mimicry – so much so that it would have been impossible to record the process in its entirety. During my time in Java I acquired a very basic understanding of Betawa Indonesian grammar and a vocabulary of maybe a hundred and fifty words; the natives are able, by frequent contact with traders, to carry out certain transactions in English: between us, therefore, with mutual good-will we were usually able to reach an understanding, mainly on matters to do with operations on the plantation, but also with basic social interactions, such as asking after a man's health, or the welfare of his wife and children, giving thanks and praise. My conversation with Garwyn was of a similar nature to this.

The dialect contained some grammatical features with which I was not familiar at all, as well as items of vocabulary that I found obscure, though, as I have said, most of the tangible things, like the hut, the dogs, the beakers could be easily comprehended by pointing, as could, by mimicry, some of the more universal concepts like pride, love, anger. The word *stranger* with which he first addressed me, was something like *man not of Affalach,* and he referred to womanly beauty, or specifically a beautiful woman, as when he spoke of Branwen, as *woman with the face of the bright moon,* though also, at one point, he referred to her as *woman who is the keeper of the cauldron of life.* The descriptive elements of his dialect, if I am not mistaken, borrow elements from spiritual and celestial concepts, and the operations of the natural world frequently seemed to have connotations of magic.

Affalach, I concluded, incidentally, does not refer specifically to the settlement, but more broadly to the territory over which the tribe has influence, and it seems to have connotations of fertility as much as being a land defined by geographical boundaries. When I told him – my very first attempt to communicate – that I had come from the area of the river, I used the Welsh word *afon* which had an immediate meaning for him, though when he suggested the alternative *aber*, meaning, of course, *estuary,* it was my nodding of the head that led him to conclude that I was a member of the crew of one of the visiting boats.

His stories were scattered with references to the time of the ancestors, the time of the giants, the time of the floods, but I suspect that there was no clear sense of chronology in his narratives, and he seemed to have no difficulty believing that Bran, the son of Llyr, and Branwen's brother, was both a giant and a man. When I asked a question aimed at clarifying how tall Bran was, or how long ago it was since there were giants on the earth, he would try to answer, but more often than not, in frustration at my ignorance, he would say, "wait for the celebration, and listen to the bards. They know. They remember everything from the beginning of time."

He would grin and raise his cup and we would let it pass. He was perfectly happy, on the whole, I think, to believe he was talking to someone who simply had a different dialect, and a certain level of non-comprehension did not trouble him at all.

After we had parted, and when I had left the village, I found my coat and boots, where I had hidden them, and then made my way back towards Llyn Coron, anxious not to be overtaken by darkness on my way home. From the lake, I looked back once towards the harbour and the settlement, now hazy in the evening light. Then, I made my way up beyond the lake to find the path.

A few minutes later, as I hurried on, with my head leaning forward over my steps. I heard a deep rumbling sound, like that of thunder. I looked up, and just below, in a steep sided cutting that was suddenly before me, a locomotive engine burst into sight, pumping billows of smoke and steam up into the sky.

Chapter 14

It was not easy to find the opportunity to speak to Bryony alone. In the early days of my convalescence, when I was confined to bed, it was quite natural for her to be in my room as a nurse, and again, quite natural, as I became fit for social interaction, for incidental conversations to take place between us.

It would not have been seen as proper, however, now that I was up and about and, to all extents, recovered, for a young woman of the house to be in my room, however innocent the purpose, at the same time as myself. During the evenings of poor weather at the beginning of June, we became accustomed, as I have already said, to sit in the parlour, Bryony, Megan, Llwys and myself, and we did so still, and though the conversation there was pleasant enough, it was not a context for any exchanges of a personal or private nature.

There was, in addition to this – or at least I felt it to be the case – a sense that Bryony wished to avoid me. If I noticed, to begin with that she sometimes appeared moody and self-pre-occupied, our continuing acquaintance seemed to have made her more at-ease, to smile at greeting, or just in ordinary situations where our eyes happened to meet. Now, however, she seemed to be on her guard at every moment, walking with her head bowed to avoid any direct contact of her eyes with mine, and making sure that there was always another person with me in the room before she herself entered.

This continued for three or four days, and it was then, one Saturday morning, that the weather changed suddenly again, and I woke up to find the beautiful warm light of a summer morning streaming into my window. I dressed immediately, before the rest of the household was about, and walked, first to the sea-shore and then to my favourite point on Llyn Maelog. It was beautiful morning, with the sun drawing scents from the grass and the flowers and herbs beside the path, promising a hot day in prospect; such a morning where it was impossible not to feel invigorated, where even the most nagging of preoccupations dissolve for a time in the pure pleasure of existence.

Though, of course, it is in the nature of such pure and simple happiness that it cannot last more than a moment. Even as I breathed in the scented air, and felt the light wind on my cheek, and heard the soft murmur of the distant surf, a voice began to whisper in my ear, telling me that my time in Rhosneigr was drawing to a close. I was too well, now, to prevaricate any longer with my father, not unless I wished to tell an outright lie, and I knew that whether I liked it or not, it was not the life of a poet or artist that awaited me, but that of a small wheel in the great machine of commerce that was so much my father's pride and joy.

As if to compound my returning sense of the uncompromising nature of reality, I was met, outside the General Store, as I made my way back, by Mr Hughes, who handed me a letter from my father. As soon as I was back in the privacy of my room, I opened the letter. Once again, I could detect the deliberate attempt to avoid impatience, though as with my father's actual speaking voice, the more it was disguised, the more it showed. He said, however, that he hoped I was feeling better, that he would certainly have come to visit me had not a bout of rheumatism attacked him in the recent poor weather. He went on to say that there was an important reception in Slane, County Meath, to which we were both invited. He would be sorely disappointed, he said, if I did not attend. The date appointed for this social event was a week away.

At the thought of having to mix, in what would be, no doubt, a sumptuous setting, with Ireland's best, my heart sank. My father was a man of few social pretensions himself, more at ease with his plantation bosses, his factory managers and his shipping agents than he was mixing with hereditary landowners and titled gentry, but he had a successful man's ambition to be acknowledged by such people of rank as their equal, and it was an ambition which he was determined that I share. Whatever my inward protests, however, I knew that I had no alternative but to obey.

I kept to my room for three hours, at odds with myself and with the world. It was only the sight of Llwys, going out to tend his bee-hives in the paddock behind the house, just after lunch, that brought me round. I went out into the garden where the earlier promise of a glorious afternoon was now fulfilled. The house itself seemed empty, and I felt a sudden sureness that if only I could come across Bryony now, the conversation I had been wishing for could take place. In the scullery, with his feet up on the corner of the table, reading a newspaper, was Evan.

"Gone to Holyhead," he said, anticipating my question, but not looking up at me. "Megan and Bryony. On the train. Gone to do some shopping. Fancy a pint?" he added, the cadence of his Welsh accent somehow touching a perfect note of mockery.

I mumbled my excuse, and went out again, following the path to the seashore. The tide was fully out, and a thousand sea-birds were feeding along the strand on what the sea had left. The skeleton of the *Norman Court*, still visible, though a little diminished each day was almost close enough to walk to. I went to within thirty yards of her, seeing that the tangled metal was already showing pock-marks of rust and corrosion. I had no desire to go any closer.

I dreamed that night of horses, this time a real dream, with horses as great as giants thundering through a railway cutting and beating up the dust, galloping as if from some terror which pursued them.

When I awoke once more, to the dawn of another beautiful day, I wrestled with my thoughts for a good while, and decided at last that come what may, I was going to seek an opportunity to broach the matters that had been so much in my mind, with Bryony.

Chapter 15

Later that morning, the family set out, as they did every Sunday, to go to the early service at church. My mother was a devout church-goer, and until her death, going to the service each Sunday had been a regular part of my life. I enjoyed the quiet atmosphere of the day of worship, the call to service which came from several different churches in the vicinity, their bells overlapping, the musty smell of the church with its hint of incense, the stained glass windows, the organ pipes, the silver eagle on the pulpit. My actual religion I took for granted, to a large extent; it was a set of beliefs I had been brought up with and didn't question, a moral code which I believed to be virtuous. After my mother's death, the cosiness of habit slipped somewhat, and my father, a reluctant church-goer himself, did not rebuke me over this. Being abroad, in the east, gave me insights into humanity which challenged some of my complacency, and seeing the way other societies practised their worship gave me a more detached perspective on my own. Nevertheless, for two or three weeks, since my recovery, I had accompanied the family to church as a mark of deference to their hospitality, and had rediscovered, in that plain and unadorned church, close to the sea, some of the simple pleasures of being at worship. Though not all of my pleasure was entirely virtuous: the sight of Evan, uncomfortable in his best Sunday suit and starched collar, sweating and squirming at each reference that the minister made to sin, retribution and eternal damnation was, I admit, to my own shame, a cause of some private satisfaction.

The church had a small reed organ, with a high piping sound, much less grandiose than the church organs I was used to, and it was Mr Hughes, the shopkeeper and postmaster, who was the regular organist. As we entered the church that morning, he was playing as usual, a basic hymn melody which he elaborated and decorated with his own playful trills and tropes. We moved to the usual pew, and Bryony, I noticed, made haste to be the first to enter, so that I, respectfully bringing up the rear of the party, would be prevented from sitting next to her. Llwys sat next, then Megan, then Evan, and as Evan did not particularly have the welcoming look of one who wanted me to sit next to him, I slipped into the empty pew behind.

I listened, with pleasure, to Mr Hughes' continuing extemporisation as the church filled, reflecting privately that I could well prefer listening to his playing for the full length of the service, but at last he drew his piece to a close, and the minister began. I changed the direction of my gaze to look towards him, and found that the line of view to the pulpit brought Bryony's profile, from where I was sitting behind, immediately into my field of vision. To all intents and purposes, I was concentrating directly on the minister; secretly, and, I admit, a little furtively, the true focus of my eye was her. She was completely still, her face expressionless as far as I could judge, but I was able to see, in the light from the window, the finest of down on her cheek, and I was fascinated to watch, at regular intervals, the blinking of her lashes, and the occasional slight movement of her lips, as if she was, half-consciously, preventing them from dryness.

What the service was about, the text, the sermon, the liturgical references, I cannot tell you. I was slightly ashamed of my covert scrutiny of Bryony's face, but I could not help myself. It was only as the service drew to a close that I noticed that one of her gloves, which she had set beside her in the pew, had fallen to the floor. My usual instinct would have been to pick it up and hand it to her with a gentlemanly courtesy, but instead, seeing the possibility of a pretext for speaking to her alone, I left it where it lay, and as we shuffled out of the pews to join the rest of the congregation leaving through the church door I hoped that she would not see it or realise that she had lost it.

I nodded my appreciation to Mr Hughes as he played on to the congregation's exit, and shook the minister's hand outside the church door, ostensibly a virtuous worshipper, but all the time, feeling the excitement of my less than virtuous scheme.

I waited until we had walked a good way, a hundred yards or so, from the church, and then said, "Bryony, you're holding your gloves, but are you sure you have them both? It looks like only one to me."

She immediately checked and confirmed, as I knew she must, the absence of the other glove. "I must have dropped it," she said.

"I'll run back and get it for you," I offered.

"No," she said, obviously not wanting to be in any way beholden to me. "I'll run back myself. It'll only take me a minute. You all go on."

She set out.

"We'll wait for her here," said Llwys, much to Evan's annoyance, evidently wanting to get home as soon as possible, to get out of his starched collar.

"You go on," I suggested. "I'll walk back and meet her."

I saw Evan looking impatiently to Llwys.

"Very well," said the old man, with a sigh, obviously feeling the pressure of his look.

I made my way quickly back towards the church, determined to make the most of the opportunity which had at last presented itself. Bryony came out of the church, saw me, and stopped for a moment, and then, resigned that she could not now avoid me, came on, so that we fell into step together.

"Why have you been avoiding me?" I asked.

"It's for your own good," she said, not refuting the accusation, as she might have done, with an evasion.

"How can it be for my own good?" I countered, with an attempt at lightness.

"You must go back to your proper life. Your life in Ireland," she said sadly. "That's for the best."

It was, I realised, an admission that there could be, or possibly was already, however unspoken, something between us.

"Who is Efnisian?" I asked.

She stopped, and turned to me, with alarm in her eyes.

"You mustn't ask me that!" she said emphatically.

She walked on quickly ahead. I hurried to catch her up and drew her elbow back until we were again in step together.

"I was there," I said. "You saw me, twice, and recognised me. I need to understand what happens."

"You can't understand it," she said. "I don't understand it. I can't explain it to you."

"But why can't we talk about it?"

"Because it won't help. It's better for you if you just go."

I didn't tell her about my father's latest summons.

"Perhaps I should ask Llwys or Evan. Maybe they can tell me something."

"No!" she said with sudden alarm.

I didn't say anything else. I felt I had been cruel enough already. We walked on for a while in silence. Then, it was she who spoke.

"We can't talk when other people are in the house."

"No," I agreed.

"The day after tomorrow," she continued, after some moments' thought, "my father is to take us to the market in Llangefni. We go every month or so. He may ask you to go with us, but you must make an excuse. Say you're going to Holyhead again, to make arrangements for your journey home. I'll wait until the morning and then feign a sickness to stay at home. You must set off for Holyhead, and book your passage in good faith, then come back early. So long as you have made your arrangements you will not have told a lie about your purpose. That may give us a little time for the conversation you want."

"What about Evan?"

"He'll be at work. He doesn't usually come home at midday, and if he thinks there's no-one here, he certainly won't. He'll go to the tavern to quench his thirst."

By now we had almost reached the garden gate, and the others, just ahead of us, were going into the house. At the very last moment before we joined them, she squeezed my fingers conspiratorially as if to bind me to the secrecy of our assignation.

Then she walked ahead of me, into the house, and I heard her sharing the success of her mission to find the lost glove with Megan.

Chapter 16

I slept uneasily that night. To begin with I felt guilty for the importunity by which I had forced Bryony to agreeing a clandestine meeting, and all the duplicity that went with that. At the same time, recalling Llwys' words, such a short time ago, about hospitality, I tasked myself with the accusation that my arrangement to meet his daughter privately, whilst he was away from the house, amounted to a betrayal of that trust. I lay awake for a long time, whilst sleep eluded me, and as different strands of thought passed over my mind, like rags of cloud across the moon on a windy night, I wondered if Bryony, too, was lying awake, troubled, as I. Her room was just along the landing, down three stairs and along a short corridor with two doors, the other door being that of Megan's room. For a moment the mad thought of going to her door to listen, and see if she was restless too, swept over me, but I dismissed it, summarily, for the madness it was. Instead, I listened intently, but there was nothing but the sounds of the house itself, the night-creaking of stairs and doors, an intermittent drip of water, and outside, the distant call of an owl. I remembered the nights spent on the *Norman Court* when, even in fair weather, the ship was alive with the creaking and groaning of masts, and the sound of the wind like a deep low exhalation in the sails. I went to the window and looked out to where, in the blueness of the night, the rocks of Cremlyn Bay were just visible, a deeper shadow, and somewhere out there, though too indistinct from the darkness to see at this hour, was the tangle of wreckage which had been brought by the same stroke of fate that had brought me here.

I returned to bed, and to my dilemma. Of course, I put it to myself, there was nothing dishonourable in my intentions. I had some right to know, surely, if anyone could tell me, what explanation there might be for the strange happenings that had befallen me. Besides, I now had it, from what Bryony had already, by her reactions, confirmed, that I was not simply in the grip of some madman's hallucination, and despite her reluctance to be drawn into conversation about it, simply to hear about her experiences must certainly throw some light on my own.

There was another course of action that was open to me, and this I also considered. This was simply to release Bryony from the obligation of speaking to me, which would no doubt be a relief to her, and therefore a kindness on my part, and take the earliest opportunity to return home to Ireland. Since these strange episodes had never happened to me anywhere but here, I felt it to be unlikely that they would follow me to any other place. In that sense, I could be free to return to my own life.

I veered one way and then the other, until at last I was quite unable to steer a way through my own oppressive thoughts. The only thing which remained constant was the recollection of Bryony's fingers gripping my own as we approached the garden gate, and it was with this image in my mind, as the light of dawn began to filter in through the window, that I eventually fell asleep.

Chapter 17

I was late rising the following morning, but seeing Llwys in the kitchen garden by the side of the house, I immediately let him know that I was to go to Holyhead the following day to make arrangements for my passage home later in the week.

"That's a pity," he said. "We are going to Llangefni, tomorrow. The market, you know. Very lively. I think Megan and Bryony would have welcomed your company, And I, of course, and I…"

"Don't put pressure on him," said Bryony, who, hitherto unseen to me, was pegging washing on the line. "He has things to do."

"You see how I am ruled by my children!" said Llwys, with wry intonation. "Are you sure you cannot delay by a day or two?"

"I had another letter from my father."

"Ah, yes, well, he will be missing you, no doubt. Well, so be it."

I felt glad that I had completed this first part of the plan, and as the rest of the day passed uneventfully by, I wondered that I had been so troubled by it the previous night. That night, at supper, Llwys rehearsed the arrangements for the next day.

"We'll be back for three o'clock or four o'clock," he said, for Evan's benefit, "so you'll not miss your dinner."

"I hope someone's going to make up some snap for me," said Evan. It was evident that, with the prospect of other people going off to have a day out, he felt entitled to make himself awkward.

"I'll make some snap for you," said Bryony.

"No, you won't!" said Megan, with sudden venom. "Why does it always have to you, Miss Goody-goody, going about as if butter wouldn't melt in your mouth!"

"Please!" said Llwys, sharply. "Remember, we are at table, and we have a guest."

"Let Megan make his snap," said Bryony, quietly. "I had no intention to upset her."

"Yes, you did."

"Please," said Llwys again.

Evan grinned smugly to himself, pleased to be fought over. The rest of the meal passed in silence.

I set out for Holyhead early the next morning, having slept soundly through the night. The rest of the household was just stirring as I left. I did not wait to take breakfast. Whether or not Bryony had yet made her excuses, I did not know, no more than I knew whether or not she and Megan had made their peace, but, to be honest, I wanted to be away from the house before that business took place.

I walked up the lane towards the railway station. It was cloudy and cool, the air moist and full of morning scents. At the station, a cart was waiting with potatoes and turnips that were going to market in Holyhead, but apart from myself no other traveller was joining the train. The carriage itself, however, was plentifully populated with people travelling to Holyhead, presumably for business or to catch the ferry.

Finding a seat opposite a fellow who said 'good morning' and who, hearing my own accent, announced himself to be a Cork man, I sat in preparation for the journey which was no more than twenty minutes. The train passed through rough heathland with a number of shallow coastal lakes, and with the mass of Holyhead Mountain ahead, gradually swinging to the north until a wider body of water appeared to our left.

"The inland sea," my companion announced.

I nodded my appreciation of his information.

"You'll see in a moment," he further explained. "The Stanley embankment."

I had seen it before, of course, on my previous visit to Holyhead, but had not known its name.

"Built by Telford. Same man who built the bridge at Menai. Thomas Telford."

Before we reached the embankment, the train slowed and stopped in a siding.

"Train coming the other way," said my companion.

Sure enough, a few minutes later the train out of Holyhead came shunting past; then, the signal lifted, and our train pulled forward through the points onto the main track, and we were off again, onto the embankment.

It was, perhaps, a mile long, and straight as a ruler's edge, joining the island to Holyhead which was, I learned, geographically, an island in itself. On the left was the `inland sea` trapped by the embankment, though with a great culvert to allow the passage of tidal water, and to the right was the open sea, bounded by a wide bay with a silting river estuary visible at that state of the tide.

"River Alaw," my knowledgeable companion said, seeing the direction in which I was looking.

I nodded again. He smiled with self-satisfaction and proceeded to relight his pipe.

"Caergybi," he announced when this operation was completed. We were now speeding past the embankment and on towards the town of Holyhead.

"I beg your pardon."

"Caergybi. Original name of Holyhead. Named after a saint, you see. Church up on the hill, there, if you've a mind to see it."

We parted at the station, shaking hands, and I made my way to the booking office of the Kingstown ferry and made a reservation for my passage on the Friday morning. This done, I found that unless I were to hurry to catch the return train already waiting to depart, I had a two hour wait before the next departure. I considered this, and though I was keen to get back, I judged it better to wait. I did not want to arrive back so quickly that it might seem I was just waiting around the corner for Llwys and Megan to set out.

I made my way along Market Street, past the bank where I had done business the week before, and up the hill to the more elevated part of the town. There, above the market and the busy trade streets, I found the church to which my fellow traveller had alluded. An ancient stone gateway led to the inner grounds, which command an imperious view over the harbour and the sea, and the church itself, which, I discovered, is undergoing some current renovations sponsored by the Stanley family [presumably the same as of the embankment] but goes back many centuries to a monastic foundation established where once the Roman legions had a fortification. A small separate chapel known as Yglwys y Bedd, or Church of the Grave, was said to contain the remains of an Irish warrior king of the fifth century, but the church suffered greatly from the ravages of the Vikings, and more latterly, those of Parliamentary troops during the English Civil War.

    I stayed there for an hour, noticing that the moist cloud cover of the early morning had now disappeared, leaving high chariots of white in a blue sky, heralding another fine summer day. On the way back down the hill, I stopped in a bookshop wondering if I might find some things to leave as gifts for Llwys, Megan and Bryony - I rather doubted that any kind of reading would be much to Evan's taste! The only thing which caught my eye, however, was a copy of 'The Tempest' by William Shakespeare. I had never read the play, but thinking its title apposite to the circumstances of my arrival on Anglesey, I decided to buy it as a gift for Bryony, hoping I would be able to find a discreet moment to present it to her. Checking the time, I now made my way quickly back to the station, and twenty minutes later, was again crossing the embankment, with the estuary of the Aber Alaw on the left, on my way back to Rhosneigr.

Chapter 18

At first I thought the house was empty, and that Bryony had changed her mind and had gone with the others to Llangefni after all. There was no sound from the kitchen or the scullery, her usual places of occupation during the day. I stood at the foot of the stairs, and listened again, wondering if, in consistency with her story, she had remained there, in her room, until my return. I waited for a moment and then went up the stairs to the short corridor and knocked lightly on her door. There was no reply.

When I went down again, I found her in the parlour, sitting in her usual place, her needle and embroidery in her hand.

"Would you like to sit outside, in the garden?" I asked.

She shook her head, slowly, but decisively.

I sat down opposite her, not knowing, now we were here, how to begin. She, too, remained silent, patiently working on at her needle. I wondered whether or not to give her the book I had bought as a present for her, but decided that it was not, at this moment, appropriate.

"You saw me there," I said at last, trying to formulate my words carefully, "you recognised me, didn't you?"

"I've never spoken of it to anyone before," she replied, obliquely.

Another silence of some duration followed. I wasn't sure whether she was simply reluctant to talk, or whether, like me, she did not how to talk about it.

"Yes, I knew who you were," she volunteered, finally.

"There are other people there, too," I said. "I mean people you know, from here."

I deliberately refrained from mentioning Evan by name, but saw her nodding.

"You see some people there, yes. They never say anything, afterwards. Nor should we."

"But why not? Why is it wrong to try to understand?"

"Because you will think that you can change things. And you can't."

"Why would I change things?"

"You would want to protect me from my fate, and that can't be done."

"What is your fate?"

"I don't know yet. I know it's something terrible but I haven't discovered it yet."

"I've seen you in two places," I said.

She nodded.

"And is your fate in both places?"

"I don't think it is in the first place. I think that is where Evan's fate is. You saw him there?"

"Yes."

"You saw what he did?"

I nodded.

She had stopped working at her needle now, and was looking at me directly and so intently that it seemed she might almost be looking through me at something beyond.

"It's as if people have done something from which they cannot escape, and so they must forever go back and live through those events again."

"Is my fate there, too, then?"

"I don't know. You will find out. Or maybe, when you go back to Ireland it will trouble you no more. That is what I tried to tell you, coming back from the church. That is what I hoped."

"But why?"

"Because I didn't want you to be trapped, like me. Also," she added, "I didn't want you to talk to my father or Evan, because then we would lose the peacefulness of our household."

"How often does it happen?"

She shrugged. "Sometimes once or twice in a month, sometimes more, I don't really know how it works."

"And is it just those two places you go to?"

She shook her head, and I waited for her to continue in her own time.

"The other place is worse," she said, at last. "I was terrified there and I thought that was my fate."

"What is that place?" I asked.

She stood and walked to the window so that I saw her as a silhouette against the bright light outside.

"She is in the groves of the sacred oak," she said, in an abstracted voice. "She is dressed in silken garments, and garlanded with flowers."

"Who is it?" I asked. "Who are you talking about?"

"The priests come to see her every day," she went on, as if she hadn't heard me. "They are kind to her, and treat her with great respect, but she understands that the reason for this is that she is to be a sacrifice."

It dawned on me now that the woman she was talking about was herself. It was as if, looking out of the window, she was picturing the scene as it took place, describing it in a detached way as if she were someone else.

"She is calm because she knows it is fate, the gods require a life to be given so that new life will flourish, but at the same time, she has terror because she doesn't know how long it will be, or if there will be pain. She has heard of the wicker, and of the triple-death but she doesn't know exactly what they mean. She has left her mother and father behind, and all her family. The only people she sees now are the priests, and they are the only people she will ever see again. No-one else is allowed in the sacred groves."

"What happens?" I asked, my own voice quiet as a whisper.

"That was how it went," she said, turning back from the window. "Just to there, to the terror of waiting, and that's what I thought my fate was to be. It always stopped at that point; and then, once, it started to go on…"

She sat down in her chair, and took up her sewing again.

"She wakes up, one day, in the sacred grove, and that day, the priests are not there, Usually they are there before she wakes, and when she goes to sleep, but on this day there is no-one there. She waits, and waits, but no-one arrives. And then a terrible temptation comes over her to escape. She isn't confined because she has always known that it will be futile to attempt any escape, but now she is overcome with the desire to run away and to live, and so she begins to run.

"And as she runs she is even more terrified than when she was there, because she knows that if she has chosen the wrong direction she will run into a clearing where the priests are waiting, or even worse that she will hear the sounds of pursuit.

"At last, she comes out of the wood on the brow of a hill looking down a steep slope towards the sea. Opposite is the mainland, and there is a moment of gladness in her heart because she recognises the mountains as those she can see from her home. Then, she sees that from the distant shore, boats are putting out. At first it seems like just a few, but as the few get nearer, there are more and more behind, and then more and more, until it seems to be an entire navy of boats, and then she sees that there are horses too, bearing armed men, swimming the shallow waters of the strait.

From below her now, on the near shore, she hears a strange shrieking. She edges closer. The shrieking is from women, their hair loose to their waists, naked, and with their bodies smeared with the blue dye of warfare. The priests are there, too, uttering strange prayers and curses, holding torches of fire high above their heads, and chanting as the wild women dance, inciting the warriors, who stand in a thick line on the shore to do terrible deeds of bloodshed on the approaching foe.

"The sun glints from the boats as they approach, and the reflection is from the metal coats and helmets which the enemy soldiers are wearing. As they reach the shore, now just fifty yards off, she sees that they are young men, some of them just boys, and that their faces are pale with fear. But their generals shout commands to them in a strange language, and they splash from the boats into the shallows, and then a terrible slaughter begins. The warriors of the island are no match for the silver-clad army coming from the mainland, and soon the sea is awash with their blood.

"They retreat with the women and the priests to a higher field and stay to defend themselves there, but now the horsemen with their armed riders have joined the foot soldiers and they wreak havoc, slaughtering men and women and priests with no mercy. After an hour they are all dead, their bodies strewing the ground, and the silver-clad soldiers go foraging for more people to kill.

"She hides, and waits until nightfall, and then, timidly, and sobbing all the time, she tries to make her way home. In a village she comes to, they tell her that invaders have come to destroy the priests, but that they have killed indiscriminately, old men and women, children and babies, spreading terror, quashing any resistance. They have set fire to the sacred groves, they tell her, the oak woodlands are belching fire and filling the air with smoke.

"Does she get back home?" I asked.

"When she awakes she is at home, and she wonders if it is her fault. If her sacrifice had been completed, life for life, perhaps the island would have been spared such terrible slaughter. But then she realises that that is not her fate, as she thought it was, but that her fate is in a different place."

"And does her fate lie in Aberffraw?" I asked, discreetly picking up on her mode of telling the tale.

"I don't know. It may be."

"What happened, after she went through the gate, when I was following her?"

"They told her that the obstacle to her marriage had been removed," she said, and then turning to me suddenly, "how did you know about Efnisian?"

"Someone told me about him. That he was jealous of her marriage, or offended, I'm not quite sure, I couldn't understand him perfectly."

She nodded, but said nothing further to elaborate.

"So what happens next?" I prompted.

"The preparations for the marriage begin. They dress the hall with garlands of all flowers which can be found in Affalach, and begin to prepare for a feast. Poets and storytellers are summoned from all parts of the kingdom, and festivities are planned. Special garments are woven from the finest threads, brought from the furthest places our ships have travelled to. Pavilions are made to accommodate Matholwch and his chosen men in the courtyard of the royal enclosure whilst the festivities last. And then..." She looked up at me from her needle work, and shrugged. "I don't know what then. It may be that for her it ends there and her fate is somewhere else after all."

A short time after she had finished, as we both sat in thoughtful silence, there came the sound of the garden gate latch opening, and a moment later, Megan's high-pitched laughter.

Bryony stood and moved to the door, and then turned back towards me. "Whatever happens," she said, "you must not interfere, or try to do anything to change things. Promise me this. Everything that happens is something that must happen. Promise me this?"

I nodded and she quickly reached out her hand, offering it to mine. Then, she went to the door, and I heard Megan's voice. "We came home early. I couldn't bear to think of you being here ill on your own."

"I'm much better now," said Bryony.

"I'm sorry we fell out. It's all my fault. Do you forgive me?"

"Come on you two!" said Llwys. "I'm parched for a cup of tea."

"I've brought you something," said Megan. "I can't wait for you to open it."

Their voices trailed away, into the scullery. I waited for a moment and then slipped quietly up the stairs to my own room.

Chapter 19

The heat of the afternoon persisted into the night, and the next day was even hotter. The sea was flat and listless, and such waves as there were flopped lazily onto the shore, as if the very last stage of their journey was hardly worth the effort. Above the indistinct horizon, the light shimmered in a bright haze, harsh to the eyes, and over the distant mountains the blueness of the heavens modified to tense thunderous grey.

The doors of the forge were kept open all day, and inside, Evan could be seen, in his leather apron and gloves, wiping an arm over his hot grimy face. Rivulets which usually drained quickly to the sea, ran sluggishly, giving off a faint dank smell of decay. Outside the general store, the postmaster fanned himself with the lid of an empty biscuit tin, and laughingly told passing customers to come back another day, as he had no intention of moving from where he was.

By Llyn Maelog, insects teemed, their noise a vibrant hum of woven sound, and now and then, over the water there was a plop where a fish had just taken a fly, and ripples spread out from the point in small circles. In the surrounding fields, the labourers, turning and tedding the mown grass, leaned longer on their forks, wiping sweat from their brows, and as the day approached its hottest hour, in the early afternoon, the fields were empty as they sought half an hour's respite in the shadows.

I walked restlessly from one place to another, sitting for a short space here, and a short space there, but unable to settle. Two days remained before I was to leave for Ireland, and that, as much as the oppressive weather was the cause of my restlessness. The conversation with Bryony had been both a beginning and an end; the element of subterfuge had lent a certain excitement to our private meeting, but now that was over, and as the hours dwindled towards my departure, I felt the inevitable disconnection from Rhosneigr, and from Bryony, drawing near.

Despite the heat, I decided eventually to walk as far as Aberffraw again. The little town, on the gently rising hillside, was asleep in the afternoon sun. I walked through, trying to picture the route I had taken when I followed Bryony, the king's enclosure, Garwyn's hut where the lovely Ceri had washed my hands, and given me mead and blueberries for refreshment – but the layout of the buildings and streets, no doubt overlaying others of previous centuries and settlements had long destroyed the natural contours of the land, and the silting of the estuary had made the hill seem lower and more modest than I had seen it when I followed her, Bryony or the girl called Branwen. I stood in the town square, and tried to imagine the brightly decked hall, the pavilions in which the guests from across the seas were to sleep, wondering if, indeed, Branwen's fate had been sealed there, amidst the ancient rituals of her tribe, but the quiet streets gave me no reply.

I crossed the river by the stone bridge to the rough heath and the sand flats. The tide was out and the water course was little more than a shallow stream, just deep enough in the channel for a rowing boat. Following the path, I walked out towards open beach where the river meets the sea. Over the mountains now, the air was a dun grey, the colour of lead, and as I stood there, a distant rumble of thunder could be heard. The prospect of a storm somehow pleased me, even though I was an hour's walk from home. It was not just the thought of it clearing the air, but the anticipation of a violent and dramatic display.

I was not disappointed. A cool wind now came in from over the sea, tossing up the waves, and the thunder clouds strode out from the mountains like an approaching army. A flash of lightning turned the sky to sepia, and an awesome silence was followed by a sudden crack of thunder, reverberating like a relay of tight explosions, and then the rain started, pummelling the sand like grape-shot.

Already soaked to the skin, I took shelter in the recess of a sand dune overhung with turf, and watched. The sky had now darkened to an almost midnight hue, but was alive and tormented with the disturbance of the storm. It lasted for an hour, as if the centre of the tempest had anchored itself over the bay of Aberffraw, and then gradually, the intervals between the flashes of lightning and the bolts of thunder lengthened, and the darker clouds began to move away towards the horizon.

Before me now the tide was high up on the shore, and the warm air had returned. When I turned back towards the estuary, the channel was full and deep, and on the far side, underneath the hill, a flotilla of ships was riding at anchor.

Chapter 20

Along the horizon to the west, the setting sun was now visible in bloody streaks seen through rents in the storm cloud, and the dusk over the hill of Aberffraw was tinged with violet. With the tide at the slack of high water, the estuary was full, and perhaps seventy or eighty yards wide at the point where I now stood.

After the heat of the day, I could think of no more refreshing a prospect than to swim to the opposite shore, but after my recent experience of the perils of the element, and with the disadvantage of a weakened shoulder, it was not without apprehension that I stood contemplating the risks of such a venture. The alternative, I calculated, would mean finding my way back on this shore, probably as far as Llyn Coron, where the river could be crossed, for I knew that the bridge, in this state of the water, would be immersed under the flood, if, indeed, it was there at all.

I considered, too, that soon the light would be failing, and with this now a main factor, for I had no wish to be trapped in the darkness on a deserted stretch of shore, I decided at last to commit myself, and to rely on my own strength. I stepped into the water. Under my feet the sand was a sludge that slipped between my toes, and I felt my feet sinking to the ankles, but the bank was steeply shelved, and I was soon able to push out into the deeper water. As soon as I felt the coolness of the water slipping over my flanks, I felt a sense of freedom and exhilaration. My shoulder worked well, and without pain, and with each stroke I saw the opposite shore drawing nearer.

As I drew near, the masts of the ships loomed above me, and then, as I was directing my strokes to come to the bank between two of the hulls, I heard a man's voice calling, "There you are, at last! Where have you been?"

I knew immediately, from his accent, even before I saw the red bandanna, that it was Paolo.

"Where have you been!" he repeated, with some exasperation, as he took my arm, helping to pull me out of the water onto the deck of the boat.

"I was on the other shore," I said. "I was caught by the storm."

."What a time to go for a swim," he said, now laughing, "though no doubt you wish to be fresh on this of all nights!"

"What do mean?"

"No time for questions now. Get yourself dry, it's high time you were ready."

"Ready for what?" I asked, five minutes later, after he had sat me down on a chair and put a sheet around my neck.

"Keep your mouth closed," he warned, "or you'll find it full of shaving soap! And keep still if you don't want your throat cut."

He proceeded to shave and dress me, talking incessantly. "Just feel that against your skin," he said, helping me into a robe that was, indeed, as soft and cool as silk. It was dark green in colour, with a fine tracery of gold and silver circles embroidered on the breast.

"Right, now this," he continued, indicating an surcoat of woven flax, the colour of ox-blood, brushed to give it a close even nap, and with white animal fur around the collar and the sleeves.

Slippers of pale calf-skin, stitched with gold thread, a bracelet of polished bronze for each wrist, a necklace of amber gemstones, and a gold ring with a setting of delicately inlaid oyster shell, completed my attire.

"There," said Paolo, at last.

"I hardly recognise myself. Now, are you going to explain the occasion to me?"

"It's what you came to this island for," he said.

A short time later, accompanied by a dozen others from the ships, all finely dressed, we were walking up the sloping path, through the gate of the lower palisade, in the direction of the royal enclosure. It was just the same as on my last excursion. I began to understand what the occasion was.

"You can let me do most of the talking," said Paolo, as we walked on. "The dialect here is different, a little strange."

"I have spoken to some villagers," I replied, wondering whether I might see Garwyn and Ceri at the festivities.

"Well, just be careful. We must make sure, tonight of all nights, that there are no misunderstandings, no careless phrases that may be misconstrued."

"Is that because of Efnisian?" I asked, testing the water.

"He's a testy one, for sure. In the best of circumstances, these alliances can be awkward, but he'll be on the lookout for trouble, if you ask me. We mustn't give him any ammunition, and hopefully Llyr and Bran will keep him in check. Right, we're nearly there, are you ready?"

"Greetings Lord Matholwch, son of the Giant Race of Eirean, King of all its people, Master of the seas, and friend to all the people of Affalach, husband to Branwen, daughter of Llyr, and Princess of the Land of the Great…"

In all that followed, I felt a curious sense of detachment, like an actor in his role, standing outside the illusion he creates, nervous of the attention that is on him, but trusting his art and his wits to get him through. With Paolo there beside me, with his tactful hints and promptings, I managed to keep up my role without the mask slipping.

The hall was lit with oil lamps and clusters of tallows suspended from the roof. The roof beam and columns were entwined with ivy and holly, and other evergreens, whilst, just as Bryony had described, there were garlands of many different flowers, arranged to create a tapestry of colour, with sapling oak and willow trees in great bowls, cast in bronze and decorated with patterns of entwined leaves.

The bride was sitting at the far end of the hall, wearing a dress of plush scarlet, trimmed with ermine, and a silver coronet which held in place a muslin veil. Whether or not she was Bryony, the Branwen I had seen before, or some other, I could not tell. There was an empty seat beside her, to which I was now led, with a place for Paolo at my right-hand side. The other figures soon became clear, Llyr, the bride's father, Bran, the King of the Land of the Great, as he was announced, and other members of the household, and elders of the tribe. I was glad to conclude, after my introductions and acceptance into the gathering, that there was no face I recognised.

When we were seated, the first part of the celebration began. This involved contests between warriors armed with swords, wrestling and other trials of strength. Then, together, the warriors carried out a dance of war, to the beat of a drum and the music of pipes, and after that, girls and youths, in costumes that represented birds and animals, performed a dance of courtship, bringing posies of flowers, and bronze bowls of oil and sweet herbs to place at the feet of the bride.

Then came the brief formalities of the ceremony. Paolo stood and took the oyster-shell ring from my finger, handing it to Bran; Bran came forward and took a simple ring, gold and with a polished blue gemstone, from Branwen, and gave it to Paolo. Then he placed the oyster-shell ring on Branwen's finger, and Paolo placed the blue gemstone ring on mine. A fellow in a long white robe, presumably a priest, then stepped forward, placed our hands together, my right hand over hers, and tied a scarf loosely around; finally, he took a goblet containing some dark crimson liquid, and poured it over the scarf. The scarf was then removed and placed in a silver cup with a hinged lid which was then closed and sealed, to be taken, as Paolo later explained, to the sacred lake, in which, according to their custom, it would be thrown.

When all this was done, there was a great noise of cheering from the door, where people of the village were gathered, and it was said that bonfires were to be lit, and feasting was to ensue.

Our own feast began shortly afterwards, at long tables that were brought to us, dishes of meat, clay baked leg of goat, duck and chicken roasted on spits, and the eggs of small fowl and other delicacies, cooked shellfish and eels, mackerel and flounder. There was a pudding of fresh bilberries and honey, with other preserved fruits, goat cheese, and cordials of elderflower and apple, together with the mead I had already sampled at Garwyn's hut.

When the feasting was concluded, it was the turn of the poets, who told stories of battles and great deeds, and of the Gods and the Giants, and the time of the flood, in their strange warbling voices and to the accompaniment of a reed pipe. The greatest poet amongst them was an old man called Elfwch, and he told this tale of the cauldron of life.

Once, in Eirean, there were two great giants. Llassar and Kymideu, who was his wife, and if Llassar was huge and horrid, and ugly to look upon, his wife, Kymideu, was greater than him by far in all these attributes. And one day, they came to the court of Prince Vran, and Llassar had a great cauldron on his back. "We come to seek your hospitality," said Llassar, "and we know you will not deny us quarter and sustenance." "And what is that great cauldron you carry on your back?" asked Vran. "The cauldron of life and death," replied Llassar. "Each warrior killed in battle, placed within, will come forth a fighting man again, though he may not speak, and by this means may any king maintain his power against his enemies be they never so mighty." So Vran gave quarter to Llassar and Kymideu in his own halls, and for a year they dwelt there in harmony and peacefulness. But after a year, they began to make themselves hated by their drunkenness and brawling with the people, and their abuse of the king`s nobles and their ladies, and they made representations to Vran and urged him to rid the kingdom of this scourge. So Vran commanded Llassar and Kymideu to quit his lands, but they would not obey him, and because he knew that no warrior could defeat them in combat, Vran caused a chamber to be made of the strongest metal which his smiths could forge, and when it was made Vran invited Llassar and Kymideu to feast and carouse within the chamber, and provided them with meats and sauces and wine, and when it was known that the giants were deep in the thickness of their sleep, firewood was piled up underneath the chamber, and fire was set to it, and it was fanned with bellows until the chamber was red hot. And waking from his sleep because of the great heat, Llassar broke the walls with his great shoulders, and escaped, his wife with him, and the cauldron of life and death, and they came at last to the kingdom of Affalach, in the land of the Mighty. And knowing their malice, Bran, the Raven King, with his best warriors Bendigran and Garwyn, slew the great giant Llassar and his dam, Kymideu, and laid them under the mountains of the island, and kept the cauldron of life and death in Affalach, where it now remains, and will remain forever, for the protection of the people of the Land of the Mighty."

The tale ended to great applause, and Paolo leaned towards, whilst the noise of clapping was still too loud to prevent anyone from hearing his words, and whispered in my ear, "Don`t be tempted to claim that the cauldron rightfully belongs in Ireland. The tale demonstrates their pride, but also shows you the prestige of the alliance you are making."

He did not need to tell me.

My head was becoming light, and I noticed that Branwen had disappeared from the seat beside me. I sensed that the moment was quickly approaching when the illusion was beginning to fade, and that, as before, I would soon be finding a way back to Llwys` cottage in Rhosneigr.

"I think I need to sleep, " I said, turning to Paolo.

He patted my shoulder. "Don`t worry," he said, "there are a few eyelids beginning to droop! Wait for Bran to move first, then we can bid goodnight in a proper formal way. It won`t be long."

Sure enough, it was less than five minutes before Bran stood, and the rest of the company responded. The courtesies were formal but not elaborate. Bran and Llyr, and other members of the family present, formed a line by the door, and we, myself, Paolo, and our companions from the ships passed by, making a bow to each and extending our hands.

As we approached the door, a figure standing in the shadows there turned quickly away and disappeared into the night.

"Who was that?" I asked.

"That's Efnisian. And by the look of things, he is not well pleased."

I tried to recollect the face of the shadowy figure, but the features were strange to me. Not so the eyes, which, though they had caught mine for only an infinitesimal moment, were quite unmistakable. They were Evan's eyes.

The coolness of the air outside the hall quickly revived me from tiredness. I looked to see if there was any evidence of Efnisian, lingering, perhaps, with some purpose against me, but there was none. He had disappeared into the night. Paolo led me on, now, through the courtyard, to a place where an assembly of tents had been erected. One by one our companions disappeared into their separate tents, and at last he escorted me to one, in a separate enclosure which was guarded by Bran's men.

Inside, it was dimly lit by tallow lanterns, which showed an inner tent containing a couch with pillows, a stand with a silver ewer and basin, and a decanter and goblets of the same. There was no-one else within. I turned to ask Paolo if this was where I was to stay, or, rather, to ask him by what means I would return home, but already he was gone.

My tiredness now returning, I washed my hands and face, poured a drink, which was the same elderflower cordial as earlier in the night, and then, snuffing out the tallow, I threw myself down on the cushions, and waited for sleep.

Distantly, there was still the sound of revelry from lower down on the hill, and I now recollected the smell of wood fire in the night air outside. Closer to, I could hear the faint rustle of the tent's cloth in the light wind. I pulled a cover of soft, loosely woven goat's wool over me and a rug of animal furs stitched together, for the night was now growing cool, and closed my eyes again.

Whether or not I fell into a thin sleep or not, I am unsure, but the next thing I was aware of was that someone else was in the tent. Feeling certain that it must be Paolo, I sat up, and was ready to get up and put on my outer garments again, when a woman's face appeared in the light of a small tallow she was holding.

"Bryony…" I began.

"Branwen," she hurriedly corrected, smiling at the obvious perplexity of my expression. "Did you not see how my father welcomed you? Why all these festivities if not in your honour? I am Branwen. You are Matholwch and I am given to you in marriage."

"But you made me promise to do nothing that would change what had already happened."

"Everything that happens is something that must happen," she said, repeating her own words.

"Yes."

"Then this must happen."

"But I am not Matholwch, you know that."

"She knows no such thing," she said, and a moment later the business of our lips was no longer with words.

The first wispy strands of dawn were peeping through the heavens, before weariness and sleep at last overtook us, but when I awoke once more, even before I became aware of any distinction of time or place, it was from the most blissful state of rest, and, with the lingering glamour of the night still on me, and all my senses alive with gentleness and gratitude, I turned to her again.

When I next awoke, with the morning light now full, Paolo's hand was on my shoulder. "It's time to hurry or we'll lose the tide. You have to leave her now," he said, seeing my glance towards Branwen, asleep beside me. "She has her fate to meet, you yours."

"And you?"

"I have my fate to meet, too."

"Can I wake her to say goodbye."

"That will make it harder for you both. Let her sleep. When she awakes she will understand."

I slipped reluctantly from the bed, and put on the clothes which Paolo had brought for me. Soon, together, we were making our way down the hillside, where the last smoke from the dying bonfires rose to meet the morning mist. We passed through the lower gateway of the village, and climbed aboard a single masted skiff, with fore and aft rig, and having unloosed her, we cast off.

Outside the shelter of the estuary, a light breeze picked up the sails, just enough to move us onwards through the placid water. Along the shore, a low white mist was clinging, reminding me of scenes I had seen in the Indian Ocean, with islands seeming to rise above a mystical sea of mist. Soon, Holyhead mountain appeared ahead, and Paolo began to steer the boat between the rocks into the bay of Rhosneigr.

"This is where I must leave you," he said, at last. "I dare say you'll find your way from here."

"What would have happened if I had stayed with her?" I asked.

"It wasn't for you to choose."

"But there must be some choices."

"Don't try to change things from what they must be," he said, finally, "but when the moment arrives for you to be true to yourself, you will know it. Then you will choose."

I stood watching from the shore as he turned the skiff about. A few minutes later, he was sailing into the mist, and was quickly lost to sight.

Chapter 21

I awoke, in my room at Llwys' house in Rhosneigr, in the grip of a pervasive sadness, as if melancholy had washed through my spirits like a dye. How long I had been asleep, I do not know, but I must have lain down, when I returned, without undressing and without closing the curtains. I heard activity below, but did not want come face to face with anyone until I had put my thoughts into some semblance of order.

I knew that I could not catch even a glimpse of Bryony without there being a sharp recognition between us of what had happened in that strange world of our latest encounter, and I was unsure how either of us could contain or express such an acknowledgment. I was apprehensive, too, of meeting Evan. I had no idea of the extent to which he concerned himself with these events of the past in which he had apparently played a part, if at all, but if, as it had seemed to me so strongly at the time, the eyes of the hostile Efnisien were his eyes, then the rest of the story of that night could be no secret to him.

A steady slow rain was falling, leaving the window crowded with droplets which nudged each other, gathered, and then tumbled down the pane.

Gradually, however, the fog of my despondency began to lift, and in its place, an equally exaggerated sense of lightness and optimism now succeeded. The same things which, a short time ago, had been matters of apprehension and reluctance, now spurred me on. If Bryony were to affirm that we had married, and had consummated our marriage, in that world, it must also confirm the feelings which had been developing between us just here, in the ordinary world of Rhosneigr, and that prospect now, I admitted to myself, was a cause of some excitement.

As far as Evan was concerned, there was, I realised, very little he could do, unless he told what to others might seem a very tall story; and if his look of antagonism was a private one, for me alone, I felt quite capable of outfacing him with my own defiance.

It suddenly struck me that I had only two days before the journey home to which I had already committed myself. I washed my face and hands, for refreshment, and decided that I must act quickly. First of all I had to see Bryony and find a way of talking to her. Once I had reached an understanding with her, the rest would follow naturally.

I went down to the kitchen where I found Megan making dough for bread. She looked up at me quickly and then turned back to her work, ignoring me. I put this down, initially at least, to the fact that the chore was usually done by Bryony, and it was one which Megan particularly disliked.

"Where's Bryony" I asked, after a few moments.

She looked up again, and wiped strand of hair away from her face with a floury hand.

"You'd better speak to my father," she said, somewhat ominously, and I admit that a cold thrill of apprehension passed through me.

I found Llwys at his writing desk in the drawing room, his spectacles on his nose, sorting through some papers.

"I was looking for Bryony," I said.

"She's been called away," he replied, looking up for a moment, with, as I sensed, some discomfort.

"Called away...?"

"An ailing relative," he explained, "on another part of the island."

I nodded, wondering if he would elaborate, but he said no more."

"Nothing serious, I hope..."

"Time will tell," he murmured, "time will tell."

I sensed that he wished to be left to his business, and so I stepped out of the room and closed the door. I went into the parlour, and stood at the window, watching the rain. It seemed strange that Bryony should leave so suddenly, but not necessarily strange that she should be called to nurse a relative. Had I detected a coolness in Megan and an uneasiness in Llwys, or was it my own sensitivity?

The day passed by without any further conversation about where exactly Bryony was, or how long she was to be away. At first, I thought it quite likely that she would return by the evening, and when the rain stopped, I went for a walk as far as Llyn Maelog, and tried to plan how, in the brief moment which was probably the most I would have in which to speak to her privately – for I rather doubted another subterfuge possible or desirable – I would say what I had to say. The sun, now trying to break through the blanket of cloud, brought a warm humidity to the afternoon, and after the rain, there was a rich scent of verdure in the air, which was pleasant and soothing. It would have been nice, I speculated, had she been there, if I could have persuaded Bryony to accompany me on this walk. The speculation was, of course, idle, but it forced me to consider what exactly I would say to her, and to be perfectly honest, I wasn't sure. It was just a vague sense that, with the knowledge that was between us, something would happen.

By the time we sat down for our evening meal, it was clear that she was not expected to return, and nothing more was said. Even Llwys, normally so gracious and affable had become taciturn, avoiding the look of my eye when we spoke, even on trivial matters. It was as if there was a hush of secrecy about Bryony's absence that no-one dared to break. Only Evan seemed, in his own smug way, to be quietly enjoying the situation, and it struck me, perhaps unfairly, but strongly nevertheless, that he might have had something to do with ensuring Bryony's absence on the last two days of my stay.

Chapter 22

The following day, I set out for Holyhead on the early evening train, intending to stay overnight at the Railway Hotel and to take the first morning crossing to Kingstown. My departure from Rhosneigr was muted. Llwys came to the door and said his farewell, graciously but without warmth, wishing me a safe journey, and Megan stood at his shoulder. I felt, as on the previous day, that Bryony's absence had cast a shadow over our relations, hitherto so light and convivial.

On Llwys' instructions, Evan accompanied me to the station.

"Well, then," he said, as we waited for the train, "that's that, then. Should think you'll be looking forward to getting back home after all this."

"I'm looking forward to seeing my father," I replied, though more as a matter of form than with any real enthusiasm.

"Don't expect we'll see any more of you here, then, once you get back to your old life."

I was spared the need to reply by the arrival of the train, chuffing and hissing as it drew to a halt. I mounted the steps and turned to nod my goodbye to Evan.

"Oh, I nearly forgot," he said, reaching up to hand me an envelope. "Llwys asked me to give you this."

He turned to go, and I saw him ambling down the station approach until his figure disappeared. Apart from myself, the carriage was empty. I took a seat by the window and immediately opened the envelope Evan had given me, hoping that it might contain something to throw light on Bryony's absence, even perhaps a note from her directly. What it actually contained was the money I had asked Llwys to accept in return for his hospitality.

Chapter 23

The train gave a small lurch of forward motion and edged slowly out of the station. As it picked up speed, clouds of smoke and steam, flattening in the wind, floated past the window and drifted over the meadows adjacent to the track. Travel, I have often heard it said, is a great soother of the heart, and even in those first five minutes or so of rickety motion with the monotonous rhythmic clatter of the wheels over the line, I felt a numbness overtaking the pang of sadness I felt to be leaving Rhosneigr behind.

The train followed the broad curve flanking the inland sea, and then slowed and pulled into the siding where, as before, it waited for the outward train from Holyhead to pass. There was a last hiss of steam from the wheels, and then the engine fell silent, so that only the wind outside could now be heard.

As we waited, in the strange suspension of time that goes with an arrested journey, I fell into a reverie in which images of my stay in Rhosneiger passed over my mind's eye, the evenings in the parlour, the walks by Llyn Maelog, the conversation with Bryony over the strange encounters we had shared, the encounter which had followed that.

How long had passed before I came back to full awareness of the present, I don't know, but the train was still standing in the siding with no sign of the outward train from Holyhead. It was long enough, I suspected, for fellow passengers, had there been any in my compartment, to grow impatient and voice their irritation to the strangers with whom they were travelling.

I opened the window and leaned out, but could see no activity. The dusk was now falling quickly, and wind was blustering about the open window. I closed the window and sat down, suppressing a momentary impulse of panic. I reassured myself that the delay had no adverse significance, as my crossing did not depart until the morning, and that I would be able to get a room at the hotel however late the train was in arriving.

I looked aimlessly out of the window towards the bay which my fellow traveller of the previous journey had called the estuary of the River Alaw. What first caught my eye, in the falling darkness, was a flame moving down the hillside towards the shore. I stood and opened the window again, to get a clearer view, for the window was grimy with soot and smoke, and now saw not just one, but maybe a dozen such flames, like men carrying torches towards the shore.

Without questioning the wisdom or otherwise of the impulse which now prompted me, I opened the door of the compartment, and climbed down to the track. The whole train was in darkness, and still, as if abandoned, and when I passed the engine, there was not the least wisp or plume of steam to suggest that its furnace and boiler were in operation.

I crossed the track of the mainline, and made my way towards the lights. To my left, the Stanley Embankment stretched in its long straight line towards the island of Holyhead. Ahead, the lights were now much more numerous than before, coming and going, seeming to indicate a complicated business of activity, and where they met the shoreline, they threw up silhouettes of the masts and riggings of ships. I walked on two hundred yards, or so, until the scene became clearer. All along the shore, the ships were being loaded with horses and provisions, and on the shore itself, bonfires had been lit, and tents placed, as if an army was gathering.

I deliberated, whether to go forward or not. I was still near enough to hear the sound of the train coming out of Holyhead, and I calculated that if I heard its reassuring chuffing sound now, I could still regain the distance to my own train before it pulled out of the siding.

When I turned back to look, however, the landscape was not the one from which I had just come. Where, just a few moments ago, I had looked along the embankment, now there was no embankment at all. There was no road, no railway track. Where they had been the tidal water now flowed through an open channel from the bay of the River Alaw to the inland sea.

I pulled my cloak about me, and made my way forward, tagging behind a group of men carrying provisions, a whole pig, gutted and scalded, its trotters tied to a pole, sacks of wheat, flagons of water and ale. At the shore, a man directed them towards the gangway of a ship, and they disappeared on board with their load.

"What's going on?" I asked the fellow who had given them directions.

"War with Ireland. Haven't you heard?" he said, impatiently, turning away to his business.

The flaming torches had been tied aloft on poles, throwing a strange glimmering light along the shore. Everywhere, men were hurrying back and forth, at their business, stocking the ships with food and weapons. Above the din, the whinnying of frightened horses could be heard, as they were dragged and cajoled reluctantly aboard.

On a hill above the bay, a bonfire had been lit, a beacon, I presumed, to guide those approaching to the mustering point, and at lesser fires on the shore, cauldrons of broth, and spitted meat, were being cooked. I was passing one such fire when I heard a voice calling to me.

"Hey, you! What are you doing here?"

The voice was questioning rather than aggressive, but nevertheless, the fact of being challenged caused me a certain alarm.

"What happened? Did you get left behind?"

I stepped closer to see the speaker, and realised, with both pleasure and surprise, that it was Garwyn.

"Come and sit here," he said, patting a stool beside him. "It wouldn't be good for you if anyone else recognised you. Irish sailors are not in great favour just now. You're not a spy are you?"

"Just a curious observer," I said. "What happened? I thought it was peace and goodwill between your people and the Irish."

"Not any longer. As you see, war. The ships will go with the tide, an hour before dawn."

"Are you going?"

"Not me. Would that I could, but the old bones are too stiff these days, more's the pity. But I've come this far to see my son go off. There are many like him hungry to do deeds that the poets will sing of. But what happened to you?"

"I fell sick," I replied. "Hardly knew if I would live or die. One of your families here took care of me. I haven't been home to Ireland since I last saw you."

"You've missed everything then?"

"Yes."

He made a noise in his throat, as if it were too long a tale to tell, but after a moment, and after he had thrown some fresh wood onto the fire, and stared thoughtfully at the licking flames, he began.

"We all knew of Efnisian's antipathy to the match, but no-one thought he would go the extremes he did."

He spat into the fire, and shook his head. I waited for him to continue.

"On the night of the wedding feast, he went to the stables where Matholwch's horses were being kept, and took out his anger on them. Cut off their ears and their eyelids, their tails, and their lips, right back to the teeth. Dreadful business, bad enough in itself, but no greater an insult to a prince could be imagined! It was near enough war then, I can tell you. Had it not been for some of the wiser councillors on both sides, the River Ffraw would have been red with blood.

"Eventually they came up with a solution all sides could agree on. Profuse apologies, of course, Efnisian denounced by his father and Bran, and in addition, and this is what clinched it, the cauldron of life, the one brought here by the giant Lassar, to be given as a gift to Matholwch, and taken back to Ireland."

"And so, the rift was healed?"

"Yes."

"And Matholwch took Princess Branwen home with him to Ireland."

"Yes, that's right."

"So, how has this war come about?"

"Well," he said, spitting into the fire again, "that's just the beginning of the story. Here, have a drink."

He handed me a jug and I took a mouthful. It was hot and bitter to the taste, but after a moment its warmth began to spread into the blood.

"We heard nothing for a while, and assumed all was well. Then, word came back that Branwen had borne Matholwch a son. Even better! Efnisian eventually found his way back into favour, and life seemed to have gone back to normal.

"Now it seems, contrary to all hope and expectation, that Matholwch's kinsmen and advisors, hearing of Efnisian's reconciliation, began to spread evil reports of Branwen and the insult which Matholwch had suffered in Cymri, and Matholwch himself, sensing the anger of his people, deprived Branwen of her privileges as a queen, and banished her from the pleasantness of her life at his court. Instead, he had her confined to the kitchens where she was forced to take on the meanest and most degrading chores.

"Well, all this might well have gone on unbeknown to us much longer than it did, but Branwen, ever resourceful, taught a starling to speak, and told it of the whereabouts of her brother, and this starling came across the sea to Bran, and sang the tale of Branwen's woe into his ear.

"The rest you can no doubt work out for yourself."

I took another sip from the jug which he offered me, and reflected on the story he had told.

"Is Bran here?" I asked.

"He will arrive soon. A special ship is being prepared for him. After all, you wouldn't expect a giant to sail in a normal ship, would you, now?"

"Do you think it possible that I could get a passage on one of these ships?" I asked. "I will go as a soldier, of course, in service to Bran, to fight for the honour of Branwen and to bring about her safe return."

I don't know quite what inspired me to make this proposal, or what I expected might come of it, but Garwyn quickly brought me back to reality.

"I can understand your wish. Any man wants to return to his native land. But as for your desire to fight on Bran's side, think carefully. No man can fight against his own countrymen without remorse. And I fear for your safety, too. If any man were to find out who you are, it would be your death."

He touched me on the shoulder, and handed me the jug again. "This is not your war to fight, my friend. Take another drink to warm you, and then go your own way."

I recalled Paolo's words, when he spoke to me on the morning of my return from Aberffraw, *Don't try to change things from what they must be but when the moment arrives for you to be true to yourself, you will know it. Then you will choose,* and I knew that Garwyn was right. This was not my war, not my moment to choose.

I bade him farewell, and left him by the shore as the preparations for war continued. I walked back, towards the embankment and did not look back.

The engine and its carriages were still there in the siding, hulking shadows against the twilight sky behind. All was still, no sound, no light, no sign of life. I found my compartment and climbed back up to my place. From the window now, the estuary of the Alaw was shrouded in the gathering dark.

A low rumbling sound, growing closer, announced the approach of the outward train from Holyhead, and at the same time a hiss of steam from the wheels of our own engine broke the nearer silence. Seconds later, the Holyhead train came trundling past, hooting its whistle. Then the signal changed and we pulled out of the siding onto the main line, on the final stage of our journey.

Chapter 24

I awoke the following morning, in my room at the Station Hotel in Holyhead, with strong feelings of apprehension about the day ahead. Despite the time honoured maxim that lightning never strikes in the same place twice, the prospect of a sea journey of any distance – and the crossing to Ireland was of some six hours' duration – filled me with dread. What I saw when I opened the curtain did not reassure me. My window looked directly out over the harbour, and even in the shelter of the breakwater, the wind was whipping the swell into points of foam. The sky over the Irish Sea was a louring grey, darkening along the horizon.

I decided to forego breakfast, and instead took a walk along the waterfront. The weather-vanes on the masts were clinking in the gusts of wind, reminding me of the ghostly noises I had heard on Llyn Maelog on that first night of my strange adventure, now over a week ago, though it seemed much longer. I followed the path above the harbour, on the opposite side to the town, and found a vantage point from where I could see the wide curve of Aber Alaw bay; the shore, a mile away from where I was standing, was bleak and deserted.

At last, I returned to the hotel, gave instructions to the porter for my luggage, and made my way to go on board the *Isabella*, a steam ship of 842 tons, which, according to the mate, who I spoke to shortly after embarking, had been running the ferry route to Ireland since 1871. He had been, he told me, until he got his present place, with the S.S. Eleanor on the run to Carlingford Loch, and that ship, he went on to inform me, had sunk near Kilkeel, in January 1881, six months after he had left her.

"So there you are!" he said. "I'm lucky. You'll be all right with me!"

Somehow, despite the lugubrious nature of some of his anecdotes, the effect was reassuring. Perhaps it was the way he chattered ceaselessly, and heedlessly, it seemed, almost cheerfully, about the sea and its dangers. He does this crossing twice a day, I said to myself, in all kinds of weathers, and he fully expects to sleep warm in his bed on land each night – then why shouldn't I?

The crossing was in fact much worse than expected. As the ship rose and fell in ever deepening troughs of sea, I observed the faces of my fellow travellers in the passenger lounge, and saw them change, one by one, from their natural hue to unwholesome shades of white and green, before, succumbing to the sickness, they ran for the deck where they clung to the rails in their misery.

In my own case, the critical moment came when I felt my stomach beginning to turn. I had experienced it often enough in the Indian Ocean and the South Atlantic, and then had been powerless to combat it. Now, however, I gritted my teeth, and held on until the moment passed. Then, I went up onto the deck, took in deep draughts of the blustery salt air, and felt a new-found sense of freedom.

I had gained my sea-legs.

Chapter 25

My father was at the quayside to meet me, and I was surprised by the warmth of his welcome.

"My boy!" he called, advancing towards me with his hand extended. He looked me firmly in the face, nodded – as if somehow I had come up to scratch – and then threw his arm about me and laughed heartily. I was entirely unaccustomed to such shows of affection.

"Bad crossing?" he asked as we walked towards his carriage.

"Not too bad," I replied.

"You'll no doubt be hungry, I suppose. You look as if you could do with a good meal. Have you not been eating?"

"I've been eating very well," I said, bringing to mind a picture of Llwys` table, simple but perfectly adequate for the satisfaction of hunger.

"Well," he said, "we'll go to the Grosvenor and have something there."

As we rode into town, he asked a few perfunctory questions about my stay in Anglesey, and nodded at my replies, but I sensed that he did not require detail; that it was a topic to be dealt with quickly, and then closed.

"I'll have some money sent to them," he concluded.

"No, don`t," I insisted, thinking of Llwys` envelope which was still in my pocket. "They are proud with regard to such things."

"Well, I shall be directed by you," he concluded, and moved on to other topics.

The Grosvenor, at seven o`clock on a Thursday evening, was a showcase for Dublin society. Men of commerce, captains of industry, bankers, civil servants, politicians from London, men of letters, gentlemen all, and, of course , their ladies, adorned the room with its neo-classical columns and ornate ceiling. A string quartet played discreetly to one side, adding their own touch of elegance to the elegant scene.

My father ordered oysters and champagne, beef tenderloin, and a bottle of claret, and though, after my six months in the East, and my time in Anglesey, I found the ambience, at first, a little strange, I was, not having eaten since the previous day, possessed of a healthy appetite. What I was not expecting at all was that fame of my misadventure aboard the *Norman Court* had spread, and at least a dozen people approached our table during the evening to congratulate me on my happy return. There was, in the celebrity status that was respectfully accorded to me, something of a naïve assumption that I had survived for a month as a kind of Robinson Crusoe, and, a little flushed with wine, I'm a little ashamed to say that I somewhat indulged their whims.

My father was keen to discuss proposals he had recently devised, with his engineers, for putting new compressors and steam pumps into the plantations in Java. When we returned to the house, he insisted on showing me the drawings, spread on two large tables in his study, and though the mechanics of the engines was outside my comprehension, I could well understand, from the knowledge I had gained from observation during my time on the island, what a difference these developments would make to production.

"There would be consequences for the native workers," I said, "but it could improve their conditions."

"Exactly. It will need to be well managed. And that's why I want you to oversee it."

"Me? But I'm not qualified for such a thing."

"Don't underestimate yourself. You've been through a lot. I have every confidence in you."

I began to understand that he had somehow gained a new respect for me, that he was treating me as a man not a boy.

"Anyway," he said, at last, "you've had a long day. There'll be time enough to talk about these things when you've had time to settle back in. Now, let's retreat to the drawing room for brandy, and then to bed."

Strangely enough, when I was finally alone in my room, I did not feel tired at all. Everything in the room was as it had been when I left, as it had been, one might almost say, since my childhood. I opened the sash, and, as I had often done in my youth, sat on the sill to look down over the garden. Already, the picture of myself on the quay at Holyhead that morning seemed remote, as much in time as distance.

My father's references to the sugar plantations and the new machinery had brought me back to the point I would have been at had the *Norman Court* carried me safely home, and it began to seem that the episode of my life which involved Anglesey, and Rhosneigr, and Llwys Llewellyn's family was already beginning to dissolve into the same mist of unreality as had closed round some of the things that had happened to me there.

Whether I liked it or not, my life was picking up at the point where I had left it.

Part 3

Chapter 26

I spent a leisurely morning reacquainting myself with the comforts and small luxuries of home, and then went to my father's study to look more closely at the engineer's drawings of the new equipment proposed for the Java estates. It was fairly obvious that certain stages in the process, particularly the crushing and milling, would be radically accelerated and rendered less labour intensive. There would, no doubt, be scope for training some of the local work-force to operate and maintain the machinery, but a question mark would hang over the future of many labourers. Not that their lives or conditions were particularly enviable, but, in an island where Chinese and Dutch influence had made sugar the dominant crop, work on the estates was one of the few means of gaining a livelihood. It was a question which, I sensed, was going to pre-occupy me greatly in the coming months. Oddly enough, given the lack of enthusiasm which had previously made involvement in my father's business something of a chore, I found myself looking forward to the challenge.

It was in the evening, when he returned from work, that my father reminded me that the reception to which he had referred in his latest letter, and which, with all the preoccupations of my last few days in Rhosneigr, I had forgotten entirely, was to take place the following day.

It was to be held at Slane Castle in County Meath, some thirty miles from Dublin, to celebrate a visit to Ireland of Sir Charles Gavan Duffy. Sir Charles was, as my father explained on the journey, an Irish poet and patriot, and an Australian colonial politician of great note. He had retired from political office to live in the south of France in 1880 and, a year later, aged 65 had married his third wife, Louise, who had already borne him two children.

"Quite a colourful character," my father observed, as we watched the Irish countryside pass by the window of the carriage.

"So he sounds."

"Interested in the Celtic revival, they tell me, but I've no knowledge of that, or interest really, but anyway, you'll find out for yourself. Talking of marriage, though…"

"Were we?" I interjected.

"Well, no time like the present. You're twenty one, nearly twenty two – it's time you thought about finding a wife."

"You don't just find them, father, it's not a game of hide and seek."

"No, I know that, and I know that you young people have strong opinions about love, and that kind of thing, but you won't get yourself properly sorted out unless you go about it in a business-like way, and the sooner the better, especially if you're going to spend a year or two in the East. You know yourself what it's like out there. It's a dangerous place for a bachelor for any length of time. Some chaps marry native girls, of course, and I don't condemn it, but I'd rather have you take a good Irish girl out there with you, and get yourself properly set up."

"And have you had the banns read yet, and am I to meet this good Irish girl before the ceremony, or are you thinking that at the altar will do?"

"You may well scoff, but I'm simply saying this. There'll be plenty of young girls of good family on an occasion like today, so keep your eyes open. They don't stay on the shelf forever, you know."

With this, he let the subject drop, and though I might have been annoyed at his clumsy attempt to meddle, I preferred simply to be amused. I understood, now, what motives had led him to accept an invitation to a social event which would probably bore him to death, and, to be honest, I was in too good a humour to let it trouble me.

Chapter 27

The Castle of Slane is set on a hillside above the village of Slane itself with a commanding view over the beautiful woodland of the valley of the River Boyne. The estate has been in the Conyngham family for over a hundred years, and the old castle's reconstruction began in 1796, under the direction of the architect Francis Johnston, who designed many of Dublin's finest Georgian buildings, including the Post Office on Sackville Street and the Chapel Royal in Dublin Castle.

How many people were at the reception, I do not know precisely, but I would say above a hundred. They included some men my father knew from the world of business, poets and men from the world of literature, including Bernard Shaw, a young writer making his name as a music and theatre critic in London, and George Moore, and for some time I was on the edge of a conversation between these two about the merits of the realist school of writing in the novel and for the theatre.

After this, for interesting as the conversation was, I had little to contribute to it, I wandered a little apart, from the great hall to the drawing room, and was quite happy to be on my own, looking at the many art works which adorned the walls, and appreciating the diverse views from the windows.

We were called at last into the great hall, and after a speech of introduction from Lord Conyngham, Charles Gavan Duffy addressed the gathering. A spry man, in his sixties, he referred, with some irony to the local poet John Boyle O'Reilly, who, like himself, had spent considerable time in the antipodes. Duffy, it seems, disillusioned with Irish politics had emigrated to Australia in the 1850s; O'Reilly, on the other hand, a member of the Irish Republican Brotherhood, had been transported as a convict for his role in the Fenian Rising of 67, had subsequently escaped and gone on to make a career as a writer and journalist in America.

His main theme, however, as my father had anticipated, was the Celtic Revival. He was fulsome in his praise of *the young men who are busy digging up the buried relics of our history, to enlighten the present by a knowledge of the past, setting up on their pedestals anew the overthrown statues of Irish worthies, and warming as with strong wine the heart of the people by songs of valour and hope.*

His speech was enthusiastically received and during the lavish buffet which followed there was considerable discussion of the issues raised. I heard people talking of Ireland finding its own voice as a nation, though I detected some nervousness, too. There were references to the Phoenix Park assassinations, which had taken place just before my departure for Java, and to the recent hangings in Kilmainham Gaol of the leaders of the Fenian *Invincibles*, who had planned and carried out the crime. Support for Irish national identity was tempered, for those of my father's opinion, by a concern for stability and prosperity, and for others who felt that acts of extremism were likely to damage the Home Rule movement which had been enjoying some support in London.

I had found myself in company with Shaw and Moore, and one or two others again, and was being amused by Shaw's witty retorts about Irish culture, when I felt a touch on my shoulder.

It was my father. "Matthew," he said, "there's someone I'd like you to meet."

He took me by the elbow, and led me across the room, to a group of people, amongst whom I recognised some of his business associates. As we approached, a young woman turned towards us. "My son, Matthew," he said, by way of introducing me. "Matthew, this is Melissa Elwood."

Chapter 28

My first impression of Melissa Elwood was a simple one. I had never before seen a girl so disarmingly beautiful. Tumbling ringlets of gold hair, eyes the most delicate shade of blue, a modest and yet wholly beguiling smile: she was a girl who, even at the very first glimpse, might cause a man to feel an instinctive yearning in the breast.

"Mr Locke," she said, extending a hand, which, bowing, I kissed.

"Miss Elwood."

"I've heard so much about your terrible ordeal," she said. "And now I have the chance to quiz you about it. I want to know every detail!"

She indicated with her arm that we might walk together, and I offered mine, compliantly, judging from the eyes that turned to us as we walked, that I had become the envy of others in the room. Even Bernard Shaw, as we passed by his group, paused in his discourse, and cast a curious eye my way.

Encouraged at each stage by her promptings and questions, I described my rescue from the *Norman Court* and my kind treatment in the house of Llwys Llewellyn, and despite my best efforts to give a plain narrative, I sensed a very distinct wish, on her part, to romanticise my adventure.

We found our way to an open balcony which overlooked the formal gardens, and sat at wrought iron garden seat. It was a fine evening with just a gentle breath of wind, refreshing after the heat of the day, and I said to her, alluding to the pleasant bubbling sound of the fountain below, the soft twittering of swallows and the softness of the closing light, that it was a perfect evening.

"Perfect," she repeated, taking up my word.

"What did you think of Sir Charles' speech?" I asked, finding the moment slightly awkward, as if portending a premature intimacy.

"I must confess," she said, "that I didn't fully understand what he meant about digging up statues. The past always seems awfully cold to me, I like the warmth of the present, does that sound terribly superficial?"

"Not at all," I said, remembering my own excursions into the shadowy and uncertain past. "The past is full of ghosts."

We sat for a few moments in silence.

"Perhaps we should go in," I said, at last.

"Yes," she said, confidentially. "We know how people talk."

I was sorry to lose her company, and found myself looking around the room, rather jealously watching for any other man who might be enjoying a tête-a-tête with her as I had.

"Well?" asked my father, with enthusiasm, coming to sit beside me.

"Well what?" I replied, playing down the obvious inference, and simultaneously realising that to be so easily dazzled by Miss Elwood probably had a little of the ridiculous about it.

"You know perfectly well what I'm talking about!"

"I take it that Miss Elwood is what you would class as a *good Irish girl*!"

"Absolutely. Why not? Good family. Good background. You'll not deny her handsome, I trust?"

"Oh no, I don't deny that. Nor, I would venture to guess, would fifty other men here tonight!"

"All the more reason to make a bid. Snap her up. She'll not be on the market long."

"Father!"

"What?"

"Is everything to be seen as a commodity in the marketplace?"

He seemed surprised that I should ask the question.

"I don't see why not. If there's something you want, you either get it or you don't. If you have rivals and they get it before you, that's bad business. What's wrong with that?"

"Nothing," I said, at last, seeing the funny side of his earnestness. "But I shouldn't like to be tedious to Miss Elwood by dominating her company at our first meeting."

"Well, at least that's a strategy. Not that I agree with it, mind you. Strike while the iron is hot has always been the precept I've favoured."

"You'd have me a blacksmith, now, would you!"

"Enough. This silly game of word-play seems to be your favourite pass-time, but don't indulge it at the expense of seeing your chances slip away. Now, I have someone to talk to about proper business, so off you go and join the chase."

I refrained from making a quip about this last metaphor.

When I saw Miss Elwood again, she was in a group comprising an older lady, and two or three girls of her own age, and a man of fifty, who I later discovered to be her father. The fact that she had not been, as my father would have had it *snapped up* by eager male company, was, I have to admit it, a source of some quiet satisfaction.

"Mr Locke!"

The voice was that of the older lady in the group. I turned and bowed.

"Melissa has been telling us of you, and we are agreed you are our modern Gulliver!"

"Hardly that, I'm afraid."

"This is Mrs O'Sullivan, my aunt" said Melissa. She introduced me to the other members of the group.

"Please join us, Mr Locke."

I accepted the invitation, and was soon rehearsing the story of my adventure again.

"And what plans do you have now that you have returned from your Lilliputian voyage?" asked Mrs O'Sullivan, who seemed to have something of a fascination for the work of Dr Swift.

"My father has plans for me to return to Java," I replied.

"To carry out great works there, no doubt."

"I hope to oversee some improvements to the sugar estates."

"Machinery?" asked Mr Elwood, whom I now recognised at least vaguely, as a business associate of my father.

"Yes. Compressors and steam engines."

"Mechanisation!" said, Mrs O`Sullivan, throwing her eyes towards the heavens. "Good Lord, when will it ever end?"

"Probably never!" said one of the others, Lydia, Melissa`s cousin, a girl of fifteen with a mischievous grin.

"Lord help us!"

"Mr Locke," said Lydia, now addressing herself directly to me. "We were saying just now what a pity it is that we are to have no dancing, tonight. Do you agree?"

"In such company," I replied, "who would not regret such an omission!"

There was a tinkle of giggling at my attempt at gallantry.

"You should come to us," said Mrs O`Sullivan. "Before you go to Java. Shouldn`t he, Thomas?"

"Indeed," said Melissa`s father, politely.

"Come to us for a weekend and we shall arrange some dancing."

This proposal met with a chorus of approval from the girls, though I noticed that Melissa herself was discreetly silent.

"Mr Elwood will write to you in Dublin. Won`t you, Thomas?"

"Indeed I will, sister," said Mr Elwood, who, if he felt embarrassment at his sister`s liberty in issuing invitations, let no sign of it show through his polite exterior.

"There now," said Mrs O`Sullivan, clapping her hands together. "It`s done."

Chapter 29

We returned to Dublin the following morning and spent a quiet day at home. My father said nothing more about the topic of marriage, or about Melissa Elwood, but there was a quiet satisfaction about his manner, and I suspected that the grape-vine had quickly provided him with information about Mrs O'Sullivan's idea for a social gathering in my honour before I left for Java.

Meeting a couple of old friends from my schooldays in town, I made discreet enquiries, and discovered that the Elwoods were an old and well connected family of Slane, going back to the Williamite concessions. They were farmers and landowners, and the present Mr Elwood had gone into shipping, which was, of course, the sphere of activity in which he knew my father.

Of Melissa, not a great deal was known. She had been brought up in the country, and sent to school in England. One of my friends, Dermot, now at Trinity studying for the law, had seen her once at the theatre in Dublin, and reported her something of a beauty, but she was not, as far as any of them knew, part of any regular Dublin set. Telling them I had met her at a reception in Slane, they teased me with my good fortune, and teased me further with what they supposed to be my intentions; I did not tell them of Mrs O'Sullivan's scheme and the prospect of meeting her niece again in a more domestic social setting.

A letter arrived, addressed from Mr Elwood to my father on Tuesday morning. It outlined the proposal for a house party at the weekend, with some entertainments for the young people, which I took to be the dancing that Lydia had petitioned for. My presence was requested.

"Are you not invited?" I asked my father.

"No, thank God!" he retorted. "But you will enjoy yourself. And think of what I said. They wouldn't invite you if they didn't think you were a good match."

"That's very reassuring to know. Do you have any certificates to confirm my pedigree?"

"Don't jest. There's nothing wrong with your pedigree. Now, I had it in mind for you to sail in September, but if there's a wedding to be got up, we can put it off until, say, November. That should be plenty of time, wouldn't you say?"

"Too much time, father. I'm sure she will be bored to death with me by then, or I of her, or both."

Despite my flippancy, I found myself forced to think with some seriousness about the kind of plan he was outlining – however clumsy his way of expressing it. I had no wish to be presumptuous with regard to the affections of someone whose acquaintance I had only just made, but in a detached way, I could see the picture he was painting: a young married couple - myself and Melissa, as it might be - setting out for the colonies, establishing a home in one of the houses on the Estate, perhaps, before long having a family. It had many obvious attractions.

On the night before my departure for Slane, it was a long time before I slept. In an odd way, my image of Melissa Elwood had become slightly unreal, and I could not bring a true picture of her face into my mind, a fact due, no doubt, to the rather forced nature of speculating a future after only a single meeting. My sleeplessness, however, also encompassed, for the first time in that crowded week, thoughts about Anglesey. The excursions I have described earlier in this tale would seem, I now saw very clearly, to any normal person, the hallucinations of a troubled or damaged mind, and I now wished that I could diagnose them so myself in order to be rid of the burden of having secrets which I could never tell with any hope of being believed.

Chapter 30

I took the train from Dublin to Drogheda and a coach to Slane, arriving in the early afternoon. The Elwood family lived on an estate of a hundred acres bordering the River Boyne, and the house, in Georgian style, had been built under the supervision of the current Mr Elwood's grandfather.

Mr Elwood himself met me in the vestibule of the house. He shook my hand affably, instructed his manservant to show me to my room, and said that I should join the family for lunch as soon as I was settled.

The room was comfortable and airy, with a view over meadowland towards a group of willows forming a line of trees along the riverside. I washed, to freshen myself up after the journey, changed into a new shirt, and made my way down to the dining room. The family, comprising Mr Elwood, Mrs O'Sullivan, Melissa and her young cousin, Lydia, rose to greet me. "This is Robert, my son," said Mr Elwood, introducing a young man of twenty three or four, tall, and light-haired, with eyes a shade of blue that immediately marked him as Melissa's brother.

"How do you do?" he said, extending his hand, in a languid and amicable manner.

"How do you do?"

"Now," said Mrs O'Sullivan, "come and sit down. I'm sure Mr Locke is hungry after his journey. Some tea, Mr Locke?"

"Thank you."

Across the table, I glanced at Melissa. Her hair was taken back from her brow and temples, and she was wearing a pale blue cotton blouse with lace trim around the collar and cuffs. I noted the features I had not been able to picture clearly the previous evening, the fresh complexion, the finely sculpted cheekbones and full lips. Sensing that I was looking at her, she looked up and smiled, showing a row of even white teeth, and it was the smile, more than anything else, that confirmed her loveliness.

"Do you ride, Mr Locke?" asked Lydia.

"A little," I replied.

"Good. We're going to ride this afternoon."

"As long as the weather holds," said Mr Elwood.

"It will hold," said Lydia. "I've issued an order."

"The trouble with your orders, Lydia," said Robert, "is that they only seem to work when you tell us about them retrospectively."

"You'd better watch out, cousin Robert, or I will order something for you that won't be to your liking at all."

"I'm sure Lydia is right about the weather," said Mrs O'Sullivan, "but if you'll forgive me, Mr Locke, I won't join you on this riding expedition. My days of sitting on a horse's back are long over."

"It's not an expedition," said Lydia, with a giggle of mockery. "We're just going for a ride."

"Even so."

"I hope you're a good rider, Mr Locke," said Lydia. "If you were to fall and render yourself unable to dance, I'm sure Melissa would never forgive me!"

"Lydia!" said Melissa. "You may try to embarrass me, but please try not to embarrass our guest."

Lydia giggled, pleased with the response she had provoked.

"I shall do my best not to fall," I said. "I should be loath to exclude myself from the dancing, especially if I may look forward to a dance with you."

At this, Lydia coloured visibly for a moment, though she took the company's mirth at her expense in good part. "I should hope no less," she said. "I wasn't going to say anything, for fear of provoking Melissa's jealousy, but that's another thing I ordered."

We set out just after lunch, and as Lydia had predicted, the weather, which had been uncertain all morning, changed for the better; the lower clouds disappeared, and stately galleons of high cloud floated across a blue heaven. We crossed the meadows and then walked in single file along the river path, under the shelter of the trees.

"You must excuse Lydia," said Mr Elwood, coming alongside me. "She sometimes provokes all of us."

"She is high-spirited," I said. "It's an attractive trait in a young woman."

"You are charitable, Mr Locke," he said with a laugh in his voice. "But if she proposes hunting tomorrow morning, we are to present a united front of opposition."

"With that," I said, "I am in complete agreement."

We dismounted at a sandy bank by a steep bend in the river, and allowed the horses to drink a little, and then, tethering them, we proceeded on foot along a winding path which led up through canopied woodland to higher ground.

This was the first opportunity I had had during the day to talk to Melissa.

"How do you like our Meath countryside, Mr Locke?"

"It's very beautiful."

"I think so, too. But like many Irish people, I always think that my destiny will be to live far away. When I was at school in England I felt a terrible nostalgia for Ireland, but I somehow knew that I would only ever go home in order to leave again."

"And do you have any plans to leave?" I asked.

"With your experience of the world, Mr Locke, you should know that a woman does not make plans but has plans made for her."

"Let me rephrase the question, then," I said, thinking fleetingly of Bryony's preoccupation with what was to be her destiny, "do any such plans exist?"

Melissa laughed lightly. "None at present," she said, "unless other people know much more than I do."

"I sincerely hope that no plans will be made for you without your prior consent."

"I shall do my best to prevent it," she said, again lightly, and I was glad of the lightness, for I did not want it to seem that we had entered a shadow-play of negotiation about what other people might have conjectured for our respective futures,

"And what about you?" she asked.

"It is not only women who have plans made for them. My father has it in mind for me to return to Java."

"And is that prospect not to your liking?"

"I haven't always relished the idea of a career in commerce, but I am learning that sometimes one has to accept things as they are."

"Surviving a shipwreck, I imagine, must change one's perspective on life."

"For a time, when I was recuperating on Anglesey, I fancied that I would like the life of an artist. But that, I fear, is not to be."

"Is that your father's influence?"

"No, simply that I can think of nothing more irksome, in the long term, than to labour in a field where one has only the most modest of talents."

"And is the work your father has determined for you in Java also irksome?"

"Oh, not necessarily. The market in sugar is growing but the methods of production are slow and old-fashioned. There is scope for improvement. Mechanisation. That is what my father wishes to charge me with."

"A worthwhile task then?"

"Oh yes, I suppose so."

"And a project of some duration, I would have thought."

"Two or three years, in the first instance. After that I'm not sure."

"Is the date set for your departure?"

"Not yet. Sometime in the autumn, most likely."

We walked on for a while in silence, both perhaps feeling that a point had been reached where the next step forward, being one of some gravity, was one for which we were not yet sufficiently prepared.

Our awkwardness was spared by Robert who came alongside us at that moment. "Father's turned back," he said. "One of us had better hurry and catch up with Lydia or we'll not be back before dark."

"I'll go," said Melissa. "Wait here for us."

"Well," said Robert, as we waited. "Turned into a lovely day after all."

"Yes."

He looked at me, and nodded, a wry humour in his eye. "If you're thinking of proposing to my sister," he said, "take my advice and do it quickly."

"What makes you think I intend to propose to her?"

"Because you'd be a fool not to."

"She's a beautiful girl, I admit."

"Beautiful nature, too. But let me tell you, you're not the only fellow to have noticed."

"Well, I don't imagine I am."

"Mind you, that's partly in your favour. She's kept aloof, so far, doesn't like being the honeycomb with the bees all swarming round. She likes you, she'll probably say yes."

"Thanks for your advice."

"It's well meant," he said, patting my shoulder.

"Yes, I know."

"Better change the subject," he said, as Lydia and Melissa appeared through the trees ahead. "If Lydia gets wind of it, we'll never hear the last!"

"So what do you do?" I asked him, as we began to walk back.

"Family business," he said. "Same as you. As a matter of fact, I plan to go to America."

"Permanently?"

"Yes. I've no hopes for the future of Ireland. We'll tear ourselves to pieces, one way or another."

"Gloomy prediction."

"We're too emotional. That makes us dangerous. We want to dig up the past and fight over it."

"What are you talking about? Politics?" asked Lydia. "Don't listen to him when he talks about politics, Mr Locke. He pretends to despise it, but in his heart he's one of the Republican Brotherhood."

"Be careful, Lydia, or you'll end up in Kilmainham Gaol."

We arrived back at the point where we had tethered the horses, and remounted. The afternoon light had taken on a rich golden tinge, and two herons flew by, following the course of the river, as we made our way back to the house.

Chapter 31

Three local families had been invited to make up the dancing party, together with a cousin living in Ashbourne and a friend of Robert from Dublin. Mrs O'Sullivan presided over the organisation of the dancing with breathless enthusiasm, whilst Mr Elwood played the genial host, moving between the guests, ensuring that the less familiar were made to feel welcome.

The first part of the evening was made up of traditional sets, to the tunes of 'The Walls of Limerick' and 'The High Cauled Hat', and others, with the whole gathering, except those who pleaded infirmity, making lines down the room, and the steps being called for newcomers by the musicians, whose instruments were the fiddle, the bodhran and the concertina.

During this, the mood of the company, somewhat tentative and subdued to begin with, quickly turned to high spirits, and by the time refreshments were taken the room was heady with laughter and excitement.

"I hope you approve of our country jigs and reels," said Melissa.

We were both sipping a glass of fruit punch which had just the slightest hint of rum.

"Indeed I do," I replied. "And I hope you'll do me the pleasure of keeping a space for me on your card later in the evening."

"We are not so formal as to have cards, Mr Locke, but I'm sure if you catch my eye at the right moment, we can come to some arrangement. But don't forget," she added, "you promised Lydia a dance, too, and I know she's been boasting of her conquest to the whole company."

"Then I must honour my promise."

She smiled archly and moved to talk to another group nearby.

I had watched her during the sets, weaving in and out of the circle, under the arms raised to make arches, and skipping hand in hand with changing partners down the line. As my turn came, I had taken her warm hands in mine, and noted the glow of her cheek and the bright laughter of her eyes. It was not surprising, I found myself thinking, that men fell under her spell, and I was no exception.

During the interval for refreshments, I was introduced to a fellow in his thirties, Thomas McClure, who, as Robert told me, was an up-and-coming politician, an ally and confidant of Charles Edward Parnell. We spoke a little of the progress towards Irish Home Rule being made in the English Parliament, but the conversation was perfunctory, and I think we were both, on this occasion, more interested in the festive part of the evening than in the hard realities of politics.

"Have you known Miss Elwood long?" he asked me.

I immediately suspected a rival.

"Not very long at all," I said, with as much insouciance as I could muster. "A little over a week."

He eyed me suspiciously. In my heady mood, and in that knowing and silent opposition that men have in these things, I think we both thought that she would choose me over him.

The second part of the evening began with a quadrille, and I kept my promise by offering my hand to Lydia and leading her to make up a couple in a group of four with Robert's friend, and the sister of a farmer from nearby Rathmaiden. I noticed that Thomas McClure was in a four with Melissa, and when the dance was finished, I made a point of asking her myself for the first of the mazurkas, and after that, the polka.

"Are you trying to dance her off her feet?" asked Robert.

"I'm trying to beat off a rival, I think."

"What. Old McClure? Don't worry about him. He's been sniffing round like a puppy dog since Mellie came back from school. She jokes about him behind his back. Ask Lydia if you want it from the horse's mouth, but not whilst the fellow's in hearing distance, mind you!"

"I wouldn't dream of it."

Reassured by this, I did not object when McClure excused himself to replace me for the second mazurka, though in the final dance of the evening, a waltz, I duly made sure that she was spoken for.

Afterwards, I felt rather ashamed of the pettiness of this business, but that did not prevent me from thinking, as I lay awake that night, of the pleasure of dancing with her. Recalling the impression of her waist, and her hand, the animation of her face, the glow on her cheeks, I fell asleep at last, pleasantly enchanted, and more than toying with the idea that before I left for Dublin on Monday morning, as planned, I would approach Mr Elwood seeking his permission to speak to Melissa, to ask for her hand in marriage.

Chapter 32

On Sunday morning, we went to church in Slane, walking down the hill, and across the old bridge, returning for lunch at the house. It was then proposed that we should make a party for an outing to the hills of Tara, ten miles distant.

We set out in two coaches, myself, Lydia and Mr Elwood in one, Melissa, Robert and Mr McClure in the second. During the morning, the sky had a covering of light fleecy clouds, with plenty of fresh sunlight peering through, but a half an hour or so after setting out, the sky in the west began to grow heavy, as if a band of rain was heading towards us from the distant Atlantic.

"We'll be lucky to escape rain," said Mr Elwood. "I wonder if we shouldn't consider turning back."

"No!" protested Lydia. "What's a little rain. If we turn back we'll all be miserable!"

"Well, as long as it doesn't worsen…"

"It won't, I've issued an order."

We passed through the village of Navan and onto the road to Kells.

"Tara was the seat of the ancient kings of Ireland, did you know that, Mr Locke?" asked Lydia.

"Matholwch," I said.

"Who?"

"Matholwch. He was an Irish king. Long ago."

"I didn't ever hear of him."

"He went across the sea, to Anglesey, to find a bride. Branwen. But then there was a war between the Irish and the Welsh."

"And what happened?"

"I don't know yet."

"Yet!" said Lydia, much amused. "Why, is it still going on?"

I laughed.

"No. I meant the person who told me this, didn't tell me how it ended."

"Oh, well. Perhaps you'll find yourself standing on the very spot where this king Matholwch and his Welsh bride used to live! Now, isn't that an adventure!"

The road continued through rolling farmland, for another three of four miles, and then, just outside the village of Kilmessan, the coachman reined the horses to a stop. This, he explained, was the nearest we could get to the hill of Tara; if we wanted to go any nearer, we would have to go on foot. Before us, the land rose to a number of low summits, some with partially wooded slopes, but covered mainly with coarse grass, nibbled close by sheep, and not marked, like the surrounding countryside by walls or hedgerows demarking the fields.

After consultation, we agreed to walk a little way up onto the slope, leaving the coaches by the roadside with the drivers.

"We should sample a little of our ancient history," said Lydia. "Mr Locke has a personal acquaintance with one of its old inhabitants."

We set off across the paddock, and came after a hundred yards or so, to a ditch surrounding the hill, eight or ten feet deep and somewhat overgrown, with nothing other than the most rudimentary of paths across. We made our way downwards, but after only a few paces the wetness of the grass and the slipperiness underfoot began to prove too much for Melissa, and she proposed to set off back and wait at the coaches.

"I think I'll have to forego my lesson in Ireland's history for today," she said, laughing, "or risk breaking my neck!"

"Well," said Mr McClure, "I, for one, think our modern Ireland more important than any ancient relics, so I will accompany you, Miss Elwood."

"I, too, will make my way back," said Mr Elwood. "And you, too, Lydia. Melissa is right, the terrain is unsuitable for…"

"I'll go on," said Lydia, interrupting. "I'm not to be put off by a bit of mud."

"I'll go with her," said Robert.

"Well, take care."

We clambered to the bottom of the bank, and up the other side, where the ground quickly became drier.

The hill now rose above us on a shelving gradient for a fifty or sixty yards, and then steeply up to an embankment, which formed an entire circle around a second ditch, and within that circle another embankment, so that the whole made an earthworks of considerable size.

The three of us stood on the first embankment, admiring the view, which towards the east looked over what, from this height, seemed a flat plain of farmland towards the coast. To the west, the clouds which, not long ago, had threatened rain, had gathered into a darker ridge, almost like a thunder-bearing wave, though it seemed to have kept its distance, as if arrested on the horizon.

"Look," said Lydia, pointing. "There they are, can you see them?"

Below, tiny in the distance, by the road, were the figures of Melissa, Mr Elwood and Mr McClure, by the coaches.

She laughed, brightly.

"Come on, let's go back," she said suddenly, starting out before waiting for a reply.

Robert looked to me, raising his eyebrows at the suddenness of Lydia's whims.

"I'd better go with her."

"I'll catch you up in few minutes," I said. "I'll just go up to the next ridge."

He nodded and waved and set off in pursuit of Lydia. Glad to be alone, to have a few moments of solitude in which to take in the gloomy atmosphere of the place, I made my way down into the hollow of the second ditch, and then to the next summit, where a stern wind, not noticeable in the shelter of the hill, now blew directly in my face.

Below me now was flat expanse of grass, encircled by the mound to make an enclosure, with a tall stone standing erect at the centre. Again I picked my way through the rough grass, down into the sheltered hollow. Moved by the strange stillness which now prevailed, I sat down on the turf, and tried to form a picture of the life that might have been here once. Had a city once stood, here, a city of kings? Was it here, in sight of where I was now sitting, that Branwen had been brought as Matholwch's bride, only to lose the favour of the people and the king, and to be, through the vengeance of her people, a cause of war? I lay back and grasped the turf, recreating the moments in Anglesey where, waking, I had found myself slipping into another world. But there was no such transition now. Only the feeling of centuries of abandonment and desolation and above, when I opened my eyes, a low rugged sky moving steadily over.

And then I felt the first smattering of rain.

When I reached the road, they had raised the hood over each coach, and we set off directly for home. After half a mile, I looked back, and saw the hill of Tara now swathed in the encroaching rainy mist which obliterated all lines and form.

Chapter 33

After dinner, that evening, we played whist, at which Mrs O'Sullivan was triumphant and then 'I'm thinking of something', and other light-hearted parlour games. Finally, we had some songs. Both Lydia and Melissa played well, and both sang sweetly. I have never credited myself with a voice, but I fancy I comported myself rather more proficiently than Thomas McClure's wobbling tenor, but amongst the men it was certainly Robert's rich baritone which stole the show.

Throughout the evening, however, my mind was only partly on the entertainment. Since the short time I had spent alone on the hill of Tara, that afternoon, a feeling of loneliness had been lodged in my breast, a kind of homesickness, not for my home in Dublin, but for Rhosneigr. For the first time since leaving, I felt a hollow longing to be back there, and above all, a yearning to see Bryony again. I had put it to the back of my mind, partly because I could do nothing about it, and partly because of the speed of other events, but now, I deeply regretted not seeing her during the two days before my departure, not having had the chance to speak to her about what we both knew.

And later, when the company retired, and the house was silent, I remembered again that intense breathing closeness we had shared in the nuptial bed of Matholwch and Branwen at Aberffraw. Had she been taken - as had I, when I saw the ships of war departing from Aber Alaw - to any further episodes in that sequence of events? Or, given her disappearance from Rhosneigr, could it be that she was lost, trapped in that episode from the past where I had last seen her, a prisoner, like Branwen in Ireland, unable to return?

Lying awake, that night, I vowed that, if I could, I would search through the labyrinth of history to find her, to speak to her, to know what happened, to know that she was well, to bring her back.

But my power to enter that territory of the past had gone, and I had only Paolo's words to guide me: *when the moment arrives for you to be true to yourself, you will know it. Then you will choose.*

The moment of choice, I realised, was upon me now. I was infatuated, as every man who met her was, with Melissa Elwood, with her beauty, her charm, her accomplishments. Had I not been shipwrecked on the coast of Anglesey, had I instead, travelled, without incident, directly home, and into the net of my father's plans, I have no doubt that I would have succumbed entirely to that infatuation.

But I could not love her.

My heart was already taken.

Chapter 34

Monday dawned with a thin veil of mist and rain over the pastures between the house and the river. I rose early, washed and shaved with the hot water the valet brought for me, and packed my travelling bag. I was not looking forward to the formalities of departure, and at breakfast there was a subdued atmosphere, as if, after a weekend of festivities, each person was caught up in private thoughts. Even Lydia, characteristically so irrepressible, was a model of quietness and restraint.

"You leave soon for Indonesia, Mr Locke" enquired Mrs O'Sullivan.

"My father would like me to go in September," I said. I did not, of course, mention the terms on which my father had allowed for the possibility of a delay.

"Is it hot in Indonesia?" asked Lydia.

"At times, very hot. And in the monsoon, very wet."

"In the latter sense then, it is not altogether dissimilar from Ireland!"

Mr McClure gave a small laugh of approval. Melissa smiled quietly, a little ruefully, perhaps. This was the nearest we came to mirth.

It was after breakfast, as I prepared to leave, that Mr Elwood asked me to meet him at his study.

He was standing at the window, and turned to me as, I entered. "May I ask you, Mr Locke," he said, taking off his spectacles, and coughing a little before he went on, "may I ask if there is any sort of understanding between my daughter and yourself?"

"Sir?"

"None?"

"We have spoken of nothing other than that which might be shared in open company."

"I thought as much. Good. I'm glad. Thank you for your earnestness."

"May I ask what reason you have for putting this question to me?"

"To satisfy a doubt, and you have put my mind at rest. The fact is this, and I will be frank with you, though I must ask you to treat it as a confidence, for the present, at least. I received, last night, a request from Mr McClure to speak to Melissa, in short a proposal of marriage. Now, I have no doubt whatsoever that she will refuse him, but in the circumstances, I feel obliged to ensure that there is no other claim on her affection."

"I see."

"He is an old friend of the family. I would not be doing my duty if I did not give him due time to speak to her, or her due time to consider."

"Of course. My own acquaintance with your daughter is very short, too short, it might well be said, to be the basis of any serious consideration of matrimony. Particularly in view of the fact that I am soon, as you know, to set out for Indonesia for an uncertain period of time. I only fear that I may have been guilty of raising an expectation concerning my intentions…"

He raised his hand. "You owe me no explanation. I have informed you that Mr McClure has made a proposal of marriage, you need make no excuse for not making one yourself. Whatever may happen in the future is matter for future consideration, but for the present the record is straight."

"Do you think I should speak to her?"

"No, why should you? You have said there is no understanding between you. You have nothing to account for. Apart from Lydia's teasing, and I dare say, my son - for Robert is not above playing the devil's advocate - there has been no speculation regarding you. Why speak to her only to confirm the absence of feelings which she does not presume to exist to begin with?"

"I will be guided by you."

He held out his hand to shake mine, and then we parted.

Half an hour later, I was being driving along the avenue, away from the house. I looked back once, and fancied I saw Melissa`s form, watching from an upstairs window, but in the thickening rain, I could by no means be certain that it was her.

Chapter 35

"What do you mean, someone else has proposed to her?" asked my father, with some incredulity.

"I mean exactly that. She has received a proposal of marriage from another man."

"Who is it?" he asked, sharply, as if he detected some villainy.

"Thomas McClure."

"Tom McClure. The political chap?"

I nodded.

"Hmph! He must be ten years her senior. And is she likely to accept him?"

"That, I'm afraid, is something she didn't confide in me."

"Dammit, I'll speak to her father."

"No, you won't."

"Don't you want to marry her?"

I think he judged, even from the briefest of pauses that prefaced the flippant retort I was composing, that there was more to this than I had so far volunteered to tell him.

"Well?"

"No," I conceded.

"You young fool!"

"Listen to me, father," I said. "I haven't spoken to you about this before because I didn't think anything more would come of it, but the fact is there is someone else, someone I met in Anglesey, and to cut a long story short, I fell in love with her."

The shock of this was enough to make him sit down.

"In Anglesey?"

"Yes."

"My God, is she with child?"

"No," I said, though wondering, not for the first time, if Branwen might have conceived a child on her wedding night.

"Am I to judge from your hesitancy in answering that question, however, that relations between you were of an intimate nature?"

"That's difficult to answer…"

"What's difficult about it? You either were or you weren't. Yes or no."

"Yes," I conceded for I knew there was no point in trying to explain the true nature of my encounter with Bryony in Aberffraw.

He took a deep breath.

"Is there an understanding on her part? Does she make any claim on you?"

"No. None."

"Well, then."

He looked at me steadily. In his simple businessman's way he wanted the matter reduced to its simplest terms so that a line could be drawn under it on the ledger.

"On what terms did you part?"

"We didn't. Not really. She was called to go to nurse a sick relative. It was all rather sudden. Then I had to come back here."

"But you didn't see fit to say anything to me then."

"No. I didn't think it necessary. It's only after a lot of thought that I'm telling you this now."

He gave a long sigh of barely suppressed impatience.

"So, what are you proposing to do?"

"I'd like to go back to Anglesey. To make sure that things are settled in a proper way. Then, if you still want it, I'll go to Jacarta."

He stood and walked to the window, with his back to me, his characteristic way of pondering things, and an indication, usually, that he wanted to be alone.

I did not see him again until dinner, and I sensed then that his mood had not lightened. We ate in silence, apart from references to ordinary matters of the day, which served only to intensify the gulf between us.

"So," he said at last, dabbing the corner of his mouth with a napkin, "let me make sure I understand this correctly. You have just had the opportunity to pay court to a young lady of excellent family and background, a young lady, moreover of acknowledged beauty, and now you choose to return to Anglesey, and throw yourself into the arms of a woman from a family of, I dare say, modest means, who is, at best, weak enough to lose her virtue to someone she can never aspire to in terms of social equality, or, at worst, someone who sees her way, by compromising you, to gain some profit or advantage."

"If you were to meet her, sir, or her family, you would not see things in this way."

"What other way is there?"

"She is gentle," I began, "and modest..."

"How can she be modest!" he interrupted, in a sudden expostulation of brittle rage. "A woman who lies with a man not her husband is not modest!"

"She believed me to be her husband, and herself to be my wife."

"What nonsense is this?"

"You must believe what I say. Her family took me in, and cared for me when I was most in need. They asked no recompense for this. Bryony was my nurse..."

"Bryony," he retorted bitterly, "so she has a name, does she!"

"She nursed me, and I fell in love with her. Had she not been called away, I think we would have spoken to each other, and to her father, and come to an understanding."

"And are you seeking my permission?"

"Not your permission. I hoped to go with your approval."

"And if I forbid it, you will go anyway?" he asked, moving from the table to the cabinet where he poured a glass of brandy.

"Yes."

He thought for a long time.

"Very well," he said at last. "Go tomorrow. Get the matter dealt with. But for heaven's sake, consult common sense before you do anything you will regret. Ask yourself if any good can come of it, for her, or for you. Don't condemn yourself to a life of misery, that's my final piece of advice. I urge you to think about it."

Chapter 36

I did think about it. Long into the night, and then, after a few hours of thin sleep, waiting for dawn to take a proper hold, I thought about it again.

The determination I had felt, two nights before, to return to Anglesey and to bring matters with Bryony to a resolution, and the accompanying sense of purpose and excitement, now seemed a pale shadow, a fragile vehicle for hope. My father's opposition was no surprise, but even so, his dismissive attitude and final note of warning left me feeling isolated and vulnerable to doubt. The only consolation was that he had not absolutely forbidden my going to Anglesey, thereby preventing me from an act of absolute defiance.

But more than my father's cold response, what I feared was the reception I would receive in Anglesey. I had left, it seemed, almost under a shadow, with a hush about the house, and myself a stranger to its cause. How would it be, I wondered, if that patient hospitality had grown stale, if my return were to prove merely tiresome?

Or worse, if I were deemed to have forfeited my right to welcome and friendship by some misdemeanour, as they saw it, in my relations with Bryony. I couldn't believe that she would feel any obligation to tell them of what had happened at Aberffraw, in what was, after all, some other corridor of existence, and yet, because it had been so real in every other sense, how could I presume to know what reflections, or regrets, it had caused her afterwards?

And, worst of all, what if my return were to be welcomed, by Bryony herself, with simple indifference?

I had only, as my guide, Paolo's words: *when the moment arrives for you to be true to yourself, you will know it. Then you will choose.*

The moment had arrived. I had made my choice.

Chapter 37

I was at the dock in Kingstown at six o'clock the next morning. As far as one could see, looking seaward, the water was grey and still, but visibility was poor, and the inward bound ferry had been delayed by a fog out at sea. In the dock itself, the water lapped in slow greasy wavelets against the hulls, and dirty foam and floating debris littered the basin.

In the hotel cafeteria, waiting passengers hid their impatience behind newspapers, and an air of uncommunicative gentility prevailed. I sipped a cup of hot milky coffee and then returned to the pier. The tug boat was being chugged in a slow circle, before being attached to our vessel. There was the usual expert calling of foot by foot and inch by inch directions, and the little boat, with its black coal smoke making a cloud above, and the brisk fussing of the men, with their stentorian voices, gave something of the cheerfulness of ordinary business to the otherwise bleak and depressing scene.

It was eleven o'clock before we finally boarded, and I settled myself on the deck, as we inched past other boats and into the open sea. Progress was slow. As soon as the land was out of sight, the fog seemed to redouble in thickness, and now and again, from indeterminate distances and directions, the bass horns of other ships could be heard sounding their warning. Peering from the rail of the bows, into the slow drifting mist, the eye was cheated, finding, as in a snow storm, nothing on which to focus, but imagining, at every moment, that the bows of another ship would suddenly emerge, bound on a course of collision and destruction. Our own fog-horn sounded, loudly, just behind me, assaulting the ear, and the sound of the engines lessened as the captain judged it necessary to reduce speed even further.

It seemed, for more than an hour, that we were completely stilled, for there was no visible evidence of motion, though the mate, who sat and talked to me for a while – most of the other passengers had sought the comfort of the lounge –

assured me that we were edging forward, and that the current was with us. He produced a hip-flask, took a swig, and offered it to me. I accepted. It was rough, cheap brandy, but even so, I welcomed the harsh fire in my throat, and then the warmth which spread slowly through my veins.

"Look," he said, at last, turning his eyes upwards, and inviting me to do the same. Above, after thirty or forty feet of mist, the slightest skeins of blue were showing, with a hint of sunlight. And a short time later, the fog began to billow and shift, revealing, moment by moment, narrow vistas of clearly defined sea. There was the sound of a bell, and the engines cranked up with a low and increasing hum, and looking down, the bows could be seen breaking swiftly through the rolling surf.

We berthed in Holyhead at four in the afternoon, and I decided to spend the night at the hotel there rather than go to Rhosneigr straight away. Perhaps it was that I thought it better, arriving unannounced as I was, to arrive in the morning; perhaps also a kind of nervous apprehension at how I would be received, made me, even at this late moment, take refuge in delay.

The next morning, however, I awoke refreshed, and with a new sense of excitement at the venture ahead. I was on the station platform by eight o'clock and half an hour later was walking down the lane from the station in Rhosneigr. Llwys was sitting in the garden, and he rose and came to meet me.

I was cheered by the warmth of his greeting, but sensed also that there was still an underlying cause of sadness which was somehow associated with me.

"And your father is well?" he asked.

"Yes. He wants me to go back to Indonesia."

He nodded. "Business goes on."

It was Megan who brought us tea, and I had already sensed, to my disappointment that Bryony was not there.

"I didn't get a chance to say goodbye to her," I explained.

"No," said Llwys, quietly.

We drank our tea in silence for a few moments, and a short time later, both Megan and Evan came into the garden.

"How long will you be staying?" asked Megan, with seemingly polite curiosity.

"I'm not sure. I'd like to see Bryony," I said, as boldly as I could. "Is she still with relatives?"

For a moment no-one replied. Then, it was Evan who spoke.

"Llandeusant," he said. "You'll find her there. At Llandeusant."

"He doesn't want to go there," said Megan.

"If he wants to see Bryony. That's where he'll have to go."

They looked at him as if had broken some agreement to maintain a silence. But Evan was insistent.

"You go to Valley, on the way to Holyhead. Then take the road to Llanfachraeth. Follow the course of the River Alaw, until you come to the village of Elim. It's not far. Ask in the village."

The mention of the River Alaw struck an immediate note, and I set out, a short time later, taking the train to the station at Valley, which was just half a mile from the siding near the Stanley Embankment, where the train had twice stopped to let the train out of Holyhead pass by. From there, I continued on foot, taking the road northwards, towards Llanfachraeth, as Evan had directed until, with the estuary to my left, and with Holyhead Mountain in the distance, the road passed over the river.

Its course ran away, eastwards, through gently rising farm fields, and following the lanes and cart tracks close by, I came after an hour to the village of Llandeusant. It was only a scattering of houses, with a mill, but I immediately wished I had asked Evan to give me more precise directions. I spoke to four people, using the few phrases I had of Welsh. They were friendly in manner, but when I mentioned the name of Bryony they all shook their head. At last, remembering that Evan had also mentioned a place called Elim, I asked directions there, and found that it was only a short distance away.

The few houses here were even more scattered. I knocked at three doors without any more success than a shrug of the shoulders. Then, a little way outside the village I came upon a farmhand leading sheep across the lane from one field to another.

"I'm looking for a young woman called Bryony," I said.

This produced look of non-comprehension.

"Bryony," I repeated. "Bryony."

Again there was a bemused look, and I wondered if the man was hard of hearing.

"Bryony," I said again, and then, I don't quite know why, "Branwen."

At this his face changed with a light of comprehension and pleasure.

"Branwen," he repeated, as if to say, why didn't you say that in the first place. "Wait!" he instructed me. He went to the gate where the first of the flock had already passed, and called. A moment later, a boy of nine or ten appeared. The man spoke to him in Welsh and I only caught the name 'Branwen' as part of his instruction.

"Come with me," said the boy, in good English and with a responsibility beyond his years. "I will show you."

He took me along a track, two hundred yards, past a clump of woodland, and then a further hundred yards past open fields.

Then he stopped and pointed. "There," he said.

I looked for a cottage or some other sign of domesticity but there was none.

"Where?" I asked.

"There," he repeated, still pointing to the same place. "Bedd Branwen."

"Bedd Branwen?"

"Yes."

He began to walk across the field, signalling me to follow.

On the far side of the field there was small mound, with a cleft stone at the centre, and a series of smaller stones forming a circle around it.

"Is this Bedd Branwen?" I asked.

"So they say," said the boy.

"Does Bedd mean a grave?"

"Yes. Do you know about it?"

"Not really. I was looking for someone who is alive."

"She's been dead a long time," said the boy, nodding towards the stone. "They say she was a queen or something. In the old times. The scholars who come here, that is. Are you a scholar?"

"No."

"They give me tuppence, sometimes, you know, for pointing out how to get here."

"Do they now, you rascal! Well, here's sixpence, and I'll double it if you can tell me where I might find a girl called Bryony. I know she's staying somewhere near here."

He sucked in his breath and pushed his cap back on his head, for all the world like an old man.

"Name doesn't mean anything. But folk are scattered about. I can ask questions for you if you like. Thruppence now, thruppence when you come back."

"What's your name?"

"Gareth."

"You strike a hard bargain, Gareth," I said, taking another sixpence from my pocket-book.

"If she's hereabouts, I'll seek her out."

I gave him the money, and said I would come back the next day, but I had already decided that I would go back to Rhosneigr and find out more precisely where Llwys' relative lived.

142

Chapter 38

I made my way back down the lanes until I came to the Llanfachraeth road, and found a vantage point from which I could recognise, along the dunes, the place where I had seen the bonfire which I had taken to be a mustering point, that night, when I had spoken to Garwyn and seen the preparations for war with Eirean.

The entire stretch of the shore was empty now, with the Stanley Embankment crossing the far end of the bay to the wooded shore of Holy Island, with the sun just beginning to descend over the mass of Holyhead Mountain, rising high and solid in the distance. A steamer, with a smudge of smoke trailing away behind, was lessening towards the horizon.

Passing through the village, I came to the bridge over the River Alaw and stood for a while, watching the sluggish stream as it meandered through the trees and scrub towards the sea. Then, on what at first seemed merely a whim, I made my way down to the track by the river and started to walk towards the shore, following the exaggerated bends and curves of the stream through the sandy marshy ground of the estuary.

It did not surprise me, however, when I reached the shore, to find, that though the setting sun had now tipped the mountain above Holyhead, there was now no sign of the embankment or any other evidence to contradict the belief I had that I was being allowed one more visit into the past.

On the shore, I began to gather driftwood, and piece by piece built up a sizeable pile, ready for a fire. I stripped the bark off some of the driest pieces, to make kindling, and finally, just as the dusk was beginning to close around, I struck a match to light a taper, and held it to the small inner pyramid I had made of the kindling and the smallest twigs. A frail flame played for a while over the surface of the bark, and then, just at the point where it seemed about to extinguish itself, a stronger flame emerged, licking upwards, and the twigs began to crackle.

Within minutes the fire had taken a secure hold, and I continued to feed it until a hot bed of glowing cinders began to form at its base and the flames began to lick eagerly upwards, cracking and spitting sparks into the darkening air above.

Then I sat and waited. The whole of Holyhead Island was now in the deepest shadow, and a pale moon had risen to the north west, casting a rippling trail of silver across the sea. The evening had started to grow chill at my back, and I pulled my coat around me, but the fire was hot on my face and on my outstretched hands.

Then I heard a call, distantly, from the direction of the sea, and as I scanned the darkness, I saw the sail of a single ship silhouetted in the trail of moonlight. It drew slowly closer, steering, it seemed towards the beacon of my fire. At last the bows scraped onto the sand, and two men jumped out, and drew the boat up as far as they could on the next wave. Other men aboard were reefing in the sail, and then joined their companions to secure the boat. Then, they made their way towards my fire, and slumped down in front of it, warming their hands. From their wounds, and bandages and their weapons, they were obviously soldiers.

"We don't know who you are, stranger," said one man, "but, for this, thanks. We wanted to make landfall before dark, but couldn't. Your fire showed us the way. We've been at sea for two days."

"Do you come from Ireland?" I asked.

"Where else?"

"Do you come home victorious?"

"We bring victory, but at no small cost."

"Are there no more ships?"

"Just one. We'll wait here until it comes. Your fire will draw it to land."

"What happened?"

"First things first! We haven't eaten since yesterday."

They brought fish from the anchored boat, skewered them and set them to cook over the fire. Then one produced a flagon of liquor, took a deep swig and passed it round.

"I was here when the ships left," I volunteered, hoping to get more from them.

The leader of the group, a tall man with a full grizzled beard, who the others called Iddic, looked at me and then handed me the flagon. I took a mouthful and handed it on.

"Did you rescue Queen Branwen?"

"You know of Branwen?"

"Yes. I know it was her mistreatment in Eirean that was the cause of the war."

"Eirean has paid for that."

"And so have we," said another.

"Branwen comes home on the next ship. With her brother Bran's body."

"He was killed?"

"Yes. He instructed us to cut off his head and to take it to the White Mount on Lundy."

"What happened to Efnisian?"

"Killed, too."

"What happened?"

"The Irish were terrified to see us," said one, now getting warm with drink. "They thought it was a forest coming to them across the sea, and when they saw Bran wading out of the water, they ran to Matholwch's court to warn him. You'd think they never saw a giant before!"

Another took up the tale. The solemn mood of their arrival had now passed, and they were enjoying their saga.

"Matholwch retreated beyond the river at Tara, and had all the bridges destroyed. But Bran wasn't to be put off. 'Let him who would be a leader, be a bridge!' he cried, and lay down over the river for the men to cross."

By now, the fish were sizzling and spitting hot oil into the fire. The men cut strips of the flesh from the bone, and handed them round. I didn't feel hungry, but took a piece anyway, and didn't realise how good the taste would be.

"Anyway," the leader resumed, "Matholwch sued for peace. What else could he do except face certain defeat? He had a house built for Bran, 'a mansion large enough for a giant among men' he called it, and promised to make Gwern, Branwen's son, the heir to all his lands."

"Branwen had a son?"

"Yes. Born nine months after the wedding, they told us. So, conceived on Welsh soil!"

The men laughed as if this were further evidence of Welsh supremacy. This news made my heart lurch, but I was keen for them to reach the end of the story. "So, was this agreement settled on?" I asked.

"It was, and all seemed well. The celebrations went on for weeks, until the mansion was completed. But treachery was afoot. Certain Irish lords, the very ones, it seems, who advised Matholwch to disgrace Branwen, hatched a plot to hide men in flour bags in the house, so that when the household was asleep they could emerge and destroy Bran as he slept. They reckoned without Efnisian, though. Ever distrustful of the Irish, he inspected the house before Bran's arrival, and detecting the plot, killed the men one by one, and threw their bodies into the fire.

"The feast for Gwern's investiture went on, but inevitably, when they were hot with wine, a row broke out, and in a fit of fury, Efnisian took hold of Gwern and hurled him onto the fire.

"Well, that was the end of the attempts to reach a peaceful conclusion. War broke out, this time with no mercy given on either side. Our forces were greatly superior, and the Irish suffered heavy losses at each skirmish. In normal circumstances, it would have been over in less than a week, but what no-one on our side was reckoning on was the cauldron of life that Bran had gifted to Matholwch to solve a previous dispute. Every Irish warrior killed in the field, was put into the cauldron, and life was restored, albeit they could not speak.

"Again, it was Efnisian, angry and controversial as he always was, who stepped in. He said that he had been cast out by Bran, and now offered his services to the Irish cause. Despite his previous deeds, Matholwch welcomed the prospect of having such savagery at his disposal, and knowing that they would take him to the cauldron if he were killed, Efnisian feigned his own death. When they were about to throw him into the caudron, he threw them aside, and before anyone could do anything to prevent it, he smashed the cauldron to pieces. It was his last act. The armed guards, recovering, and seeing his further treachery, slew him there and then.

"The war raged on, summer, autumn, winter, another spring, moving from one part of the kingdom to another. The slaughter was dreadful. Five hundred Welshmen left these shores for Ireland; we are the pitiful handful who return; the case with the Irish was worse. They would not surrender and the laws of war forced us to pursue them to the very bitter end. Of all Matholwch's people, only five pregnant women were spared. And now, the only duty which remains for us is to take Bran's severed head to the White Mount."

"The head of Bran talks," said one of the men. He was slightly wild-eyed, though whether through drink, or through the effects of his ordeal, I know not. "He talks and encourages us. He says we will go with him first to Harlech and be merry for many months, even years, before we say goodbye to him at last. I know I will stay with him until the very end."

"So will we all," said the leader, patting him sympathetically on the shoulder.

"He's right, though," said another. "Bran still has the power of speech. There's no doubt of that."

They were a strange assortment of fellows, scarred and wounded, and yet with a strong sense of comradeship, the kind that is probably best known by those who have stood side by side in combat.

"And is Branwen well?" I asked.

At the mention of her name they grew silent, none of them wanting to be the one to speak first.

It was the leader who eventually spoke. He shrugged his shoulders. "Changed," he said. "That's the only word for it. Well, for any woman to lose a son that way!"

"Fretful is how I would describe it," said another. "Hardly knows if she belongs to this world or the next."

A silence fell over the company now, each man alone with his own brooding thoughts. The fire had settled now into a glowing pile, creating a circle of warmth that enclosed us. The flagon was passed around again. I kept one eye always on the seaward side, looking for the approach of the second ship.

It appeared at last, not directly opposite us, but two hundred yards or so down the line of the shore. The men were quick to their feet and I rose to follow them.

"No. Stay back a little, friend. Until things have been properly dealt with. You have provided well for us with this fire, but this is no moment for sightseers."

"But I know the Lady Branwen," I protested. "I came here to see her."

"That may be," he said, in a manner that was firm but not unfriendly. "But her father will be there, and her sister. Let them have some private moments first."

I agreed and watched as the men approached the ship which was now drawn up on the shore. Sure enough, there was a small group of people approaching from the top of the beach.

Amongst them I recognised Llwys and Megan.

For the next ten minutes there were shadowy comings and goings about the ship. I moved a little closer, but could still make out nothing distinctly. Then, a group broke away, and began to move towards me, carrying an elaborate bronze casket, which I guessed to be the receptacle containing Bran's severed head.

"Is it all right for me to go over now?" I asked, as they passed.

They stopped for a moment and put the heavy casket down. I was glad it was covered. I did not want to see the grizzly contents, whether the head still spoke or not.

"You might not like what you see," said the leader. "She's taken it badly. Even worse now that she's back here. Blames herself. Even her father can't console her. She's not long for this world, if you ask me."

"I must go to her."

"Go then. We have our own responsibility now. We have to fulfil our sacred promise to Bran."

They picked up the casket again, and I set out towards the other group. I had gone no further than a dozen paces, however, when a blood-chilling scream made me stop in my tracks. The voice was one I recognised. It was Megan's voice and I knew what it meant.

For a good half minute, I could not move, as if a paralysis had crept the full length of my spine and legs, and then I found myself doubled over, breathing heavily, trying to prevent myself from giving way to a wave of nausea. Then I felt a hand on my shoulder. "It's all over," said the soldier's voice. "Nothing you can do now. Nothing any of us can do. You'd best go back to your home, friend. Her family will see to her now."

I sat down on the sand, and felt tears filling my eyes with the bitterness of salt. My mind tracked back to the night in Aberffraw, the night we had spent in each other's arms. And to Paolo's words the following morning, *she has her fate to meet, you yours.* This then was her fate, to die on the shore at Aber Alaw, believing herself to be the cause of the destruction of two islands. The terrible fate that Bryony had always feared. Bryony, the quiet one, Llwys Llewellyn's unhappy daughter.

When I lifted my head again, the body, wrapped in a linen shroud, was being carried away towards the head of the estuary, a man at each end of the bier on which she lay, with Llwys and Megan making a procession behind.

They followed a path beside the river, until they came to the spot where I had earlier stood on my return from Llandeusant. There was no bridge now, just stepping stones to make a ford, though as we passed, villagers, who had heard the news, joined the funeral procession, and I joined in with them.

We continued to follow the course of the river, its banks forming, it seemed, a natural route towards the interior of the island, the path marked with the hoof marks of animals, and the wheel ruts of small carts.

"There are some who have gone on ahead," I heard someone say, "to prepare the pyre."

"They say it's Princess Branwen. Is that true?"

"Queen Branwen, for she married a king."

"I never saw her."

"Nor me, though they say she was the loveliest lady in the world."

"They say that she is White Raven, and that her brother Bran and she belonged to the race of giants."

"My cousin and his sons went with them to Ireland, you know. Only one of them came back. Only sixteen. He ran away and came back with a trader two months ago. He won't say a word. Goes white when you even mention it."

We walked on, following the course of the winding stream, with the bier always ahead of us. The moon had now crossed the sky and was standing above the hills to the east, casting a pale light over the landscape, not, as I had seen it in the afternoon, fields with neat hedgerows and orchards, but rough, unreclaimed heath, with clumps of bracken, furze and thistle. A little further, and another stream joined the Alaw from the right, so that the two streams formed a kind of island between, and I began to recognise the corner of land where Gareth, the shepherd's's boy, had led me in the afternoon, the place known as Bedd Branwen.

Here, the procession stopped, and spread into a circle around a rectangular bed of firewood prepared to take the bier. The knowledge that I had seen this place before, the ancient monument of a long forgotten time, now reassured me: it was Branwen who was to be cremated here, Branwen whose ashes were to be placed in an urn by the cleft stone in the middle of a farmer's field.

Branwen.

The bier was now placed on the bed of firewood, and the linen shroud removed from the face. In front of me, people closed round to take a final look at the face of the dead queen and pay their respects. Then, they held torches to the kindling wood and the flames began to play around the bier. As the crowd backed away from the heat, I saw clearly, in the light of the flames, the pallid face of the dead girl.

It was Bryony.

The flames roared, and enclosed the bier in their fury. I wanted to scream out loud to stop it happening, but no sound came from my throat. Then, I felt the blood draining from my face and my legs, and everything became black.

Chapter 39

As I emerged from the darkness, I was gripping the turf with both hands, gripping the woody stems tightly, and twisting my fingers around them. And then the tension began to lapse, and gratefully, I felt a soft peacefulness creeping through my body. There was daylight at the window, and I was in a bed. Gradually, I recognised the surroundings. It was Llwys` house in Rhosneigr, and I was in the bedroom where I had spent so many weeks after my rescue from the *Norman Court*.

I lay there for what seemed a long time as the light gradually strengthened at the window. At first I was in the grip of considerable confusion, for I could not account for what I was doing here now, or, indeed, whether I had been away at all. So uncertain was I that had a doctor come into the room and told me that this was my first true awakening since the day of my rescue, and that I had been living in a world of illusion and madness since then, I would have believed him. It would have been so agreeably simple.

I reached for my coat, and found in the pocket, amongst the papers there, the ticket for my passage from Kingstown to Holyhead, so there could be no mistake about that. I had gone home, I had met Melissa Elwood, I had told my father that I was going back to Anglesey. I was here.

But the rest was still in confusion, and as I recalled the events that I had witnessed, on the island formed where the River Alaw met its tributary streams, my peacefulness was troubled by a deep disturbance. I could not wipe away from my memory, the vision of Bryony lying dead, her face pale and serene as the consuming flames met around her. Her fate met, her destiny completed.

I must have slept again, a thin, shallow, drifting sleep, and when I sat up, suddenly, bolt upright, it took a moment for me to realise that it was the sound of the door latch that had interrupted my slumber.

It was Megan who came into the room, with a tray.

"Are you awake, Mr Locke," she asked, with a kind of cheeky cheerfulness. "Here's some tea and some hot water for you, if you're ready. I'll leave it here, anyway, for you."

"Megan!" came a voice from the corridor outside. "Are you going to be all day?"

It was Evan's voice.

Megan rolled her eyes, with a hint of droll weariness.

"Let him have some rest," the voice persisted.

"I'd better go," she mouthed, with a humorous twinkle.

The door closed behind her, and I was left again in silence. I sat up, and swung my legs out of the bed. There was no pain, no injury. I stood up without any difficulty, and went to the window, then sat on the side of the bed and started to pull on my boots.

There was a knock on the door.

"Come in," I called, thinking how, in an instant, everything would be changed if it were Bryony; how lightly my blood would flow in my veins.

The door opened slowly.

It was Llwys.

"May I come in?"

I gestured towards the chair in the corner. He sat down.

"Drink your tea," he said. "It will stimulate and revive you."

I wanted to tell him that I did not need to be revived, but instead, I did as he said, and the hot tea was good to taste.

"How did I get back here?" I asked. "I remember nothing."

"You were brought here," he replied.

I waited for him to explain.

"You set out to find Bryony. You must have got as far as Llandeusant, and then, it seems, you lost your way. Darkness must have overtaken you. Perhaps you fainted, I don't know. Thankfully, the boy who found you was the one you had spoken to the day before. He knew you were looking for Bryony, and had come back to meet you, to tell you he had found where she was staying. It was Bryony who made arrangements for you to be brought back here."

"Is she here?"

He shook his head. "Not yet."

"Is your relative there still in need of care?"

"Her great-aunt is always glad to see her, but as you may have surmised, there was something of a deception in the story that she went purely as a nurse."

I looked at him my question.

"Bryony came to speak with me. It was she who wanted to go away. I understood."

"Was I the cause of this?"

"She thought it best that you should go back to Ireland. She didn't think that you would return. None of us did."

"But I have returned."

"Indeed. And now I think it is time you spoke to Bryony about these things yourself."

At his point, he stood, and moving towards the door, stopped to put his hand on my shoulder. "She is to come home this afternoon. You may speak to her in the drawing room, or, if the fine weather persists, in the garden. You'll not be disturbed."

Chapter 40

It was not the afternoon but the early evening when Bryony finally returned. The horse had cast a shoe, and gone lame, and had to be unharnessed and led to the blacksmith in Valley. Our meeting was postponed until after supper, and then, with Megan was in such good spirits, and talking ten to the dozen about how fine it was all to be sitting here together, I thought we would never get away.

But at last, Llwys gestured to Megan to clear the table, and, for once, Evan was a willing assistant. During the meal, Bryony and I had avoided any purposeful eye-contact beyond the usual pleasantries, but now I caught her look, and with the slightest nod of understanding, we stood, excused ourselves, and went into the garden.

It was a mothy summer night, with soft cloud like a muslin cloth above, and with the scent of stock and honeysuckle heavy in the air. We sat in the corner of the garden where I had often spent a pleasant hour in conversation with Llwys during my previous stay, and for a time, as if neither of us knew quite how to begin, we sat in silence.

It was Bryony who spoke first.

"You came to look for me at Llandeusant."

"Yes. Yesterday. Or the day before. I'm not quite sure which."

"The boy you spoke to found where I was staying. It wasn't far."

"Your father tells me it was the boy who found me."

"Yes. I sent a message with him for you and he found you."

"By the grave?"

"Yes. He said you were lying there. At first he thought you were dead."

"Your father thinks I was lost, and fainted."

"That's what I told him."

"But you know there's more to it?" I asked. "Don't you?"

She nodded, and then, for a time, we sat in silence again.

"It's difficult to talk here," she said. "Shall we walk a little down the lane?"

"Will your father not miss us?"

"I told him we might go for a stroll. He doesn't mind."

We went out of the gate at the side of the garden, and walked towards Llyn Maelog. In the perspective towards the horizon, over the sea, the clouds were heavier than they had seemed in the garden. The lake, as usual, at this time of evening, was busy with insects and swallows that swooped low over the water.

"You went back to the grave to see her cremation, didn't you?"

"Yes. I followed the procession."

She slipped her hand through the crook of my elbow, and we walked along arm in arm.

"She knew you would be there," she said. "She saw you on the shore, standing by the fire, and though it was too late for you to save her, it comforted her that you were there."

"Have you been there many times, since the night in Aberffraw?"

"Yes," she said, squeezing my arm slightly, as if to signify her understanding of the reference to Aberffraw. "I seem hardly to have been anywhere else. But I think it is over now."

"I was by the shore when the warships left for Eirean. They told me the cause of the war."

She nodded. "There was never such loneliness as she felt in Eirean. She lost her son, the son of her wedding night, did they tell you that?"

"Yes, the men told me who were returning with the head of Bran."

"She blamed herself for everything, you see. It came to seem that everything in the world that was bad, or had gone wrong, was her fault, as if she was the soil in which evil things flourished."

"But that is over now?"

"She died a long, long time ago. I don't know why she chose me to be the person who relived her story."

"When I was in Ireland, I went to a place called the Hill of Tara..."

"Yes, I know. I didn't know it was called by that name, but she saw you walking on a hillside alone; that was when things were at their worst for her, and she sent a starling to tell Bran."

"I tried to find my way back but I couldn't."

"She was longing for you to return. No," she corrected, "I'm getting confused. It was me who was longing for you to return."

We were walking now past the lake, towards the point where the stream ran through to the sea, and as I loosened the grip of my arm around hers, she allowed me to take her hand in mine.

"Why did you go away? When I came back from Aberffraw, I wanted nothing more than to see you, and you had gone."

"I was frightened. I knew what was happening between us, and..."

"You didn't trust me?"

"I didn't know if I could trust myself."

"Did you speak to Llwys?"

"Yes. At first, he was frightened that what happened to his sister would happen to me."

"Is that why you went away?"

"No. If I had talked with you then, you would have persuaded yourself to stay. But it was too close. And you were convalescing. When you stepped back and saw what was available to you in the world, you would regret your choice. That was my fear. I had to give you the chance to go away and forget about me."

For a moment, I thought about Melissa Elwood, and how near I had been to losing my head in the aura of glamour and charm surrounding her.

"I had a good chance to consider things," I said. "I chose to come back here."

By now we had reached the shore, and for a time we walked along, hand in hand, at the head of the beach, in silence. When we came to the spot opposite the remaining outline of the *Norman Court,* now, in the growing dusk, just a spidery tangle of wreckage, we stopped.

"That's the ship that brought you to me," she said.

As we stood there, a soft rain began to fall. We hurried back, and took shelter under some trees at the corner of the village until the worst of it had passed.

"Do you remember this?" she asked, holding something towards me in the palm of her hand.

It was the oyster-shell ring.

"It's the ring which Matholwch gave to Branwen."

"The ring you gave to me. Perhaps that's how I was allowed to keep it. Am I to wear it all the time?"

I nodded my head, and for a second time, with the rain pattering softly into the leaves of the tree, the business of our lips was no longer with words.

Chapter 41

It was in the throngs of people in Liverpool, two years later, that I met Evan Llewellyn for the last time. He was working as a porter on the railway station. It was some moments, in this unusual context, before we recognised each other. Despite our previous enmity, he shook my hand warmly.

"I'm working here until we have enough money to go to America," he said. He explained that he and Megan were living as man and wife, waiting to emigrate to the New World.

"I would have gone before," he added, "but she wouldn't, not as long as Llwys was still alive."

"I was sorry to hear…"

"Well, old men die. That's the way of it, really, not much more to say."

For a moment, despite his stoicism, there was a moroseness in his face which left me unable to reply. Then, quite suddenly, his cheerfulness returned.

"I was jealous, you know!" he said, with a snort of laughter. "She used to tease me about you, you know, Megan that is. Said how much she would like to nurse you if Bryony would let her. I didn't believe her of course but it got my back up sometimes, nonetheless. Should have had a better understanding of a woman's wiles, eh? Still, it came good in the end."

"We're leaving again for Java in a week."

He nodded. "It's going well, then?"

"Yes."

"And Bryony?"

"Well. Very well."

"Makes a good mother, I should think."

"Yes. And a second on the way."

"Well, now, there's a thing!" he said, his voice fraught with emotion as he shook my hand again.

"She is with me here in Liverpool, will you meet her?"

"No," said Evan, awkwardly. "It would only make us, you know, sad for times gone by. Megan will know where to write to her when we have something to say."

"I'll give you my father's address. Anything you send there will find us."

He nodded and accepted the card I gave him, putting it away in his breast pocket.

He sniffed smartly, as if preparing to say a brisk goodbye. "We must go forward not backwards," he said. "Tell her I'll always remember her fondly but there are some aspects of our past which we must leave behind – or be trapped by them."

He paused for a moment. "You'll know what I mean, I dare say."

"Yes," I replied. "I do know."

He turned to go, and then turned back and threw his arms around me in a rough hug.

It was the saddest parting of my life.

AFTERWORD

Melissa Elwood married Thomas McClure in 1887, four years after the events referred to in my grandfather's papers. A friend of W. B. Yeats [it is said that Yeats himself proposed to Melissa before he met and fell in love with Maud Gonne] and a close associate of Charles Stewart Parnell in the campaign for Irish Home Rule in the 1880s, McClure's own political aspirations were somewhat tarnished through the Kitty O'Shea scandal which embroiled Parnell, and he and his wife spent much of the next two decades in America. Aged 68, he was elected to the first Dail of the Irish Free State in 1922, though he died before taking up his seat. Eleven years his junior, Melissa remarried in 1924, an American journalist and early radio broadcaster, T. F. Hawkes [Junior]. She had two children, both girls, by her first marriage. She died in California in 1942, aged 77.

Her brother, Robert Elwood established a successful business importing motor cars to Ireland from America. He was a passenger on the *Titanic* in 1912; his body was never recovered.

My father sometimes spoke of a *Granny Llewellyn* who lived in America, somewhere near the Niagara Falls. This, it seems likely, is the half-sister of my great-grandmother, but so far as I know there has never been any direct contact between the two branches of the family.

I should perhaps add, as a final note, that sketchbooks belonging to my great-grandfather, from two different periods of his life, were found amongst the bric-a-brac which was cleared from the house in 2008. One belongs to his later years, and it is clear that he spent time during his retirement sketching the landforms and sea-scapes of the coast of Anglesey. The other is the sketchbook mentioned in his manuscript, dated 1883. On one of several pages containing sketches of Lake Maelog there is, indeed, an inset pencil drawing of a young woman, at least her face and neck; she is not, perhaps, conventionally beautiful, but she has mild and pleasing features, and dark thoughtful eyes. Underneath, in a hand certainly different from that of my great-grandfather, is written the word: *Branwen*.

The sketchbooks are now kept in a drawer in my wife`s study. Neither of them, it seems, is of anything other than sentimental value.

The end

Thank you for reading this book. If you have enjoyed it, you might also be interested in John Wheatley`s other historical novels set on Anglesey.

"A Golden Mist"

https://www.amazon.com/dp/B005IR0A82

"Flowers of Vitriol"

https://www.amazon.com/dp/B005HC6EYW

"The Weeping Sands"

https://www.amazon.com/dp/B005RO8GNM

Made in the USA
Charleston, SC
22 March 2016